JUST ANOTHER VISCOUNT IN LOVE

By Vivienne Lorret

The Season's Original Series

"The Duke's Christmas Wish" in *All I Want for
Christmas Is a Duke*
The Debutante Is Mine
This Earl is on Fire
When a Marquess Loves a Woman
Just Another Viscount in Love

The Rakes of Fallow Hall Series

The Elusive Lord Everhart
The Devilish Mr. Danvers
The Maddening Lord Montwood

The Wallflower Wedding Series

Tempting Mr. Weatherstone (novella)
Daring Miss Danvers
Winning Miss Wakefield
Finding Miss McFarland

JUST ANOTHER
VISCOUNT
IN LOVE

The Season's Original Series

VIVIENNE LORRET

AVONIMPULSE
An Imprint of HarperCollinsPublishers

Digital Edition AUGUST 2017 ISBN: 978-0-06-268561-2
Print Edition ISBN: 978-0-06-268562-9

FIRST EDITION

17 18 19 20 21   HDC   10 9 8 7 6 5 4 3 2 1

Dedicated to all the fans who thought
Ellery deserved a happily ever after.
You made this happen.
Thank you.

CHAPTER ONE

August 1825

Gemma Desmond stopped at the pond's edge and stared down at the horrid stain on her white muslin dress. By the look of the large oxblood-colored smear and trail of splotches, she might have slaughtered the wine-soaked pear instead of merely dropping it on her lap. And the poor fruit had put up quite a struggle too.

All she'd needed was an excuse to step away from the picnic, gaining a reprieve from the dreadful topic of husband hunting. She certainly hadn't intended to be so thorough.

Looking over her shoulder to the top of the hill where her aunt lounged beneath the shade of a lace parasol, Gemma felt a twinge of guilt. She loved Aunt Edith dearly. But this was supposed to be a summer holiday trip, free of plotting and planning for the next London Season.

Gemma wanted to forget, for a little while, about the reason she needed a husband.

Yet she couldn't escape it. After all, it was common knowledge that she had a mark against her name as black as her raven hair. Every member of London society knew of the evil deeds her father had done.

She was the daughter of a thief and would-be murderer. Because of that, the name *Desmond* was an iron ball shackled to her ankle, and she dragged it with her wherever she went. Even her aunt, the Dowager Duchess of Vale, had been tainted by it, losing standing among the *ton* by refusing to send her niece away. And Gemma would do anything to lift the burden from her.

Even marry a man, solely for his name.

Unfortunately, Aunt Edith had a list of helpful ideas for snaring a husband and hadn't stopped offering them since they'd left London three blessed days ago.

Now that they were in Surrey, not much had changed. Yet at least the view was different, filled with verdant rolling hills that seemed to disappear into the bright blue sky. Instead of London's brackish gray clouds overhead, white powder puffs hung suspended in place without much of a breeze to disturb them. Even the branches of the willows did not stir but hung like drowsy green pennants into the still water. Blossom-heavy woodbines grew in abundance here, scenting the air with their musky-sweet, glorious perfume.

Gemma drew in a deep breath. Before her, an oblong pond spanned quite a distance—nearly the length of a thirty-camel caravan and as wide as her cousin's townhouse in Mayfair. The place where she stood resembled a bottleneck, tapering into a gulf where the water was so clear that she could see the speckled stones on the bottom and the shimmer of apricot-scaled fish making lazy passes near the bank.

She would be content to remain in this spot for hours on end, if not for her main purpose—the pear-compote carnage on her dress.

The trick of the problem was that she was currently wearing the soiled garment. And as modern-thinking and understanding as Aunt Edith was, she likely would not approve of exhibitionism, even though they were the only two picnicking here. However, with the pond so shallow in this spot, she might be able to wade into it and lift handfuls of water to the stain.

Deciding that was her best option, she surreptitiously stripped out of her shoes and stockings, leaving them tucked together on the soft grass. Then, gathering her skirts nearly to her knees, Gemma stepped into the cool water, causing a blur of shallow ripples to break the surface.

Instantly, the cool, silky caress worked like a magic elixir designed to banish worries. A sense of peace washed through her. For that small moment, she stopped thinking about plans for the upcoming Season and the hopeless search for a husband. She even stopped her irrational worry that her father might appear and force her to leave her family again, the way he had after Mother died. Instead, she focused on the smooth pebbles beneath her feet and the ripples that gradually faded into stillness.

After a while, the sight of a curious dappled blue fish captured her attention. He didn't seem to mind or even notice that she was in his realm but swam in meandering patterns around her ankles. Unable to resist the impulse, she bent at the waist and slowly slipped her hand through her translucent reflection.

The creature suddenly stopped swimming and turned back to where her hand dangled, submerged from wrist to fingertips. She thought about offering a small waggle, pretending that her hand was the keeper of five pale worms, but quickly decided that this particular fish was far too intelligent to fall for such a ruse. And she was right. The creature did not nip at her fingers when he drew near but brushed his fin against her knuckles instead, before darting off. Then, as if to use her for a scratching post, he returned and swam around to the other side, briefly pressing his flat, scaly body against her palm. Her hand twitched from the slick, ticklish sensation and, on the mirrored surface, she caught the flash of her own smile.

In the same instant, she heard someone cough.

Startled, Gemma jolted upright. Her gaze flew to the spot where a man stood on the opposite bank. With waves of blond hair and cut, aristocratic features, he looked as if he might have stopped here shortly after descending Mount Olympus. No real man was *that* handsome.

She blinked twice to clear her vision.

Absurdly, he remained unchanged.

Standing with one leg bent, he rested the sole of his Hessian on a large mottled stone rising from the earth. And with a camel-colored coat slung over his shoulder, he had a calm, casual air about him. Then again, perhaps he was merely allowing her a moment to gather her composure, having been subjected to hordes of women struck senseless in his presence.

At the thought, Gemma recovered quickly. In her experience, gentlemen—and attractive ones at that—weren't always to be trusted.

As a matter of precaution, she calculated the distance between them as approximately ten paces across the narrow neck of the pond, twice as many if he was inclined to walk the distance along the water's edge. Certainly enough time for her to make an escape or send a shout to her aunt, who could summon the driver.

She checked over her shoulder to ensure that her aunt was still in their picnic spot. Sure enough, Aunt Edith was there, the parasol listing to one side as she offered a reassuring wave that said, "Never fear, my dear. You are under my protection."

Such a simple gesture, yet it put Gemma at ease. Apparently, Aunt Edith didn't find the man's proximity threatening. Either that or she'd already sent the driver to fetch his pistol.

"I hope you can forgive me. I did not mean to startle you," the man said, his baritone gliding seamlessly over the water without the need to shout. "I only came to enjoy the lovely view this day has brought to Dunnock Park."

He offered a smile and inclined his head in greeting, the sun gilding the tips of his hair with the movement. He was close enough that she could see the angular shadows that accentuated his cheekbones and the squareness of his jaw. The strict edge of his nose seemed to point down in a straight line to the divot above his broad mouth and to the dimple in his chin. His pale blue eyes were somehow brighter than the late summer sky and seemed to grow warmer as he appraised her in return, his gaze dipping to the water where she stood.

She looked down too and noticed she'd dropped her skirts. They were now sinking like gauzy nets around her calves. Water saturated the fabric, climbing upward, turning her petticoat and dress translucent—all the way to her knees. If she stood here a moment longer, she would have very few secrets from this stranger.

A rush of heat slid through her, and her reflection revealed the slow saturation of red tingeing her cheeks, as if her veins were flooded with Bordeaux and she was a poached pear.

"Then I shall leave the pond for you to enjoy," she said quickly, before any more of her became stained in purplish red.

Carefully, she stepped onto the grassy bank, her dress dripping and plastered to her lower legs. She did her best to squeeze out as much of the water as she could while bending toward her shoes.

"Tell me, fish charmer," he called out before she could slosh away, "would it have been better if I'd been selfish and *not* alerted you to my presence? At least then I might have learned your secret for luring fish into your grasp."

She stopped and faced him, prickled by the thought of this stranger believing her capable of dishonesty. Even if only to a fish. She'd spent most of her life bearing the weight of her father's many fraudulent schemes, even before society became aware of his deeds. Now that they knew, most of the *ton* labeled her with the same character. "'Twas no trick but a truth. The fish knew nothing of my hand, and could form no misgivings, unless through deception."

"Ah. You are a philosopher," he mused with a nod, the hint of a dimple lurking near the corner of his mouth. "I should like to hear your wisdom regarding a method to convince a certain pike—which has eluded me for years—that my hook is nothing more than a bit of silver."

Gemma felt her shoulders relax as she realized she'd leapt to conclusions. She reminded herself that she was no longer in the desert with her father and his seedy associates, or even in London, where whispers ruined reputations. In fact, thus far in Surrey, she'd encountered the best of manners and friendliest of dispositions. So it was entirely possible that the gentleman across the pond was as kind and cordial as he appeared to be.

Though only time would tell, and she had no intention of staying around long enough for him to disprove her theory.

"If I were a fish, I should care nothing for silver." She lifted one shoulder in a careless shrug. "You would do better to convince the pike that your hook is a worm in armor and requires a good bite to set it free."

He laughed at that, the sound rich and effortless, like a man accustomed to the practice. Looking across the pond, she witnessed the natural way his smile lifted his cheek, his eyes half-closed in merriment. There was no rakish gleam winking at her, nor a dark and brooding mystery in his features. In fact, his expression was open and unreserved, and he all the handsomer for it.

A whirring sensation spiraled through her in a lopsided fashion, like a winged seed falling from a maple tree. It almost tickled. And now, strangely enough, it seemed ages ago that his presence had startled her.

Not that it mattered. With the state of her clothes, she could hardly spend another moment in his company, regardless of this foreign impulse to linger.

"I wish you the best of luck in your endeavors and bid you good day," she said, detecting the reluctance in her own voice.

He sobered instantly and held out a hand, as if to stay her with an invisible thread. "Surely there are more than enough pleasant sights for us both to enjoy. And should a few words of conversation float in my direction, I would not be averse to casting my own in return."

A grin tugged at her lips, but she bit down on one corner to keep from giving in to it.

"To prove I am in earnest," he continued, "I shall sit upon the ground and keep a proper distance. Do you think your companion on the hill would mind?"

Without hesitation, he draped his coat over the stone and sank down to the grass with the effortless grace of a well-formed man who was comfortable in his own skin. And yet, he was more watchful than relaxed, as if waiting to see if she would choose to stay.

It was quite sweet. She especially liked the fact that he did not try to manipulate her. At least, no more than making it clear that he desired her conversation.

"If my aunt did mind, you would know it in an instant. She is quite formidable with a parasol." Careful with her damp skirts, Gemma sank down on one hip, her legs curled beside her, and spread the muslin out to dry. From the corner of her eye, she saw his posture relax in the way he rested his forearm on his bent knee.

He seemed to belong here, as much a part of this park as the blue and brown thrushes that were contentedly warbling from the grayish branches of a nearby beech. "I can well imagine. I was only a lad when I learned a parasol was more than shade overhead but a wooden sword with shield."

Just then, she could imagine him as a tousle-haired boy, playing the knight, and she was further charmed by him. "In the hands of my aunt, it is also a paper poker, a garden-snake flinger, and—though I shudder to inform you—a wayward bat catcher."

His dark golden brows lifted. "Indeed?"

"Open parlor windows on summer evenings do not solely allow for a cooling breeze but occasionally a chilling flurry of wings as well," she said with a grave nod, the memory still fresh from a month ago. Aunt Edith had been trying to swat the creature when the parasol accidentally opened with a *poof*. They'd both shrieked with alarm, which was likely what had stunned the flying beast enough to land inside. "My aunt caught the creature and summarily handed the net, as it were, to the butler for release in the wilds of London. By winter, I imagine he'll find his way in through a chimney."

"The butler?"

The ridiculous question took her off guard and a bubbling laugh bounded from her lips before she could think to stop it. "No, the bat. Though I do hope to see Mr. Arnold again someday too."

His smile grew. "A rather extensive catalogue of uses."

"The truth of parasols," she said, feeling that whirring inside her lungs again. It seemed to fill them, suddenly, like a hot-air balloon meant to lift her from this spot. And she almost wanted to rise into the air, solely to float across the water and land next to him.

Concealing those thoughts from her expression, she turned her attention to the water, her fingertips skating lightly over the surface.

He plucked a dark green blade of tall grass and twirled it between his fingers as he glanced down to the water too. "Would it be too bold to inquire the name of the philosopher whose teachings I shall follow from this moment forward?"

Please don't, she silently pleaded. She wanted to hold on to this light, joyful feeling for a while longer. Of the two of them, only she knew that her name was a curse that, once spoken, would end their brief acquaintance. "Too bold, indeed. My aunt would never forgive me for introducing myself to a stranger."

He scoffed good-naturedly. "But I am no stranger to Dunnock Park and, as of now, neither are you. We could just as easily have the pike introduce us." Then he glanced up toward Aunt Edith and her parasol. "There is also another solution nearby."

Was he so determined to know her name that he would climb the hill for it?

Gemma's pulse thrummed furiously at her throat—two parts anxiety and one part nervous excitement. Oh, how she wished…

"Or perhaps," she began, "since Mr. Pike is such an elusive friend of yours, and my aunt is such a distance up the hill, we might pretend that we are old acquaintances, introduced at this very spot on a late summer afternoon, quite some time ago."

He gave her another easy grin. "Ages and ages."

"To you, I am simply…Gemma." She said it quickly before she lost her nerve, but her voice was hesitant, too breathy, and might not even have reached him through the thick, honey-suckled air.

She waited for him to say that he had not heard her but then saw him mouth her name, his lips pressing together. That strange, lopsided, fluttering thing inside her took flight beneath her breast.

"And you know me as Samuel," he said, his voice hushed and lower too, as if they were sharing a secret.

Samuel. Such a nice, honest name. It suited him and yet was too formal for an introduction by the pond. After all, they were old friends now. "Yes, of course, but I have always called you Sam."

"I had forgotten." His bright, clear blue eyes fixed on her.

A blush crept to her cheeks at the warmth in his tone, and all the thrumming and whirring rushed to her head, making her giddy. She had the urge to lie back on the grass and wrap her arms around one of the fat, downy clouds overhead.

Never before had she suffered such a terrifyingly romantic notion. She was a cynic by nature, if not by upbringing. Vicious realities and a criminal father tended to keep a young woman's head perfectly level upon her shoulders and her feet firmly on the ground.

So then why was she allowing a few words from a stranger to fill her head with fluff and nonsense?

She did not know the answer. Whatever this sensation was, she had not felt it before, and did not particularly like being caught unawares. She'd learned to be more guarded than this.

At the thought, the giddiness receded in tiny prickles of sensation, like soap bubbles popping all at once. She glanced down to the water again in time to see her smile fade, the sparkle dimming in her eyes.

"I have kept my aunt too long," she said, rising to her feet and pulling her damp hem away from her legs. By the time she looked up, she saw that he was standing too and glancing to the path around the neck of the pond, as if he intended to escort her.

She shook her head. The gulf between them was much wider than he knew. "She and I have miles yet to travel before we reach our rooms."

He stopped, appearing to consider this. "Then you are merely visiting this park along your journey to…?"

"Banfern Glenn," she offered, not wanting to conceal anything more than necessary. She already felt guilty for deceiving him by purposely omitting her surname. Besides, telling him where she was staying mattered little. Once she was gone from this spot, she was certain never to see him again and to fade quickly from his memory.

The sad truth of brief by-the-pond romances.

"Ah, yes. I've heard of the village." Something just short of a smile lifted one corner of his mouth and stirred her curiosity. "From what I recall, the proprietors of the inn often hold lively assemblies in the adjacent hall. If you are going to stay in Banfern Glenn for any length of time, you might consider attending—in order to continue your philosophical studies, of course."

She wanted to smile again, but it would not reach her lips. This was it—the end of their encounter. "I do not know how long we will be in Banfern Glenn."

Strangely, Gemma wished he would insist on escorting her up the hill instead of so easily letting her go. But perhaps with such friendly manners, he often conversed with strangers and, to him, this was nothing out of the ordinary. To him, this moment would not resonate for years to come, the way Gemma suspected it would for her.

That bright gaze held hers. "Perhaps you will find an inducement to stay."

She did not know how far away the village was, but she suddenly hoped it was not too great a distance. And that perhaps she might encounter this *old friend* once more. "A philosopher would say that anything is possible."

Chapter Two

Samuel Wortham, Viscount Ellery, whistled all the way back to the sprawling brick manor house of Dunnock Park. When he caught sight of a wide-brimmed straw hat moving amidst the tall spires of crimson-speckled foxgloves and bursts of bright blue delphiniums, he took a detour to greet his favorite gardener.

The man in question held a pair of pruning shears in the grip of his gnarled hand and left a colorful clutter of spent blossoms on the ground. "Good afternoon, Father."

Edwin Wortham, the Marquess of Russford, cast a smile in his direction but continued his task. "How were the fish today?"

"Beautiful," Sam said, thinking more of the raven-haired fish charmer—with the beguiling greenish blue eyes, sparkling laugh, and shapely legs—than of the fish.

"Good. I have a taste for trout dripping with parsley butter. Your mother has been insisting on too much broth of late, and I am weary of it. How many will we be sampling for dinner?"

"Not a one, I'm afraid," Sam admitted with a shrug and bent to pick up a lavender Michaelmas daisy crowding the path. "I forgot my pole. Then once I reached the pond, I had no inclination to leave in order to retrieve it."

His father turned to him, his graying brows furrowing quizzically. "That isn't like you when you have sport on your mind."

It was true, for Sam enjoyed hunting and fishing alike—especially the latter, when that elusive pike taunted him with a flash of his spiked fins. Yet when he first spied the beauty wading in the shallows, all other pursuits fled his mind. "I was too busy pondering the truths of fish."

"Hmm. By that grin you're wearing, I'd almost think there was a girl involved."

"Can a man not grin without being besotted?" Sam asked with a laugh, absently plucking off the petals one by one.

"*Besotted*, eh?" Father's pale brows lifted like a pair of cathedral arches over all-seeing azure windows. "Now my curiosity is ripe. *Have* you met someone this very day?"

Sam dropped the naked stem and glanced to the blushing plume poppies near the arbor. He was usually more careful than this. His parents were nearly as eager for him to find a bride as he was. Therefore, whenever a young woman did catch his interest, he took his time, getting to know her character before he ever mentioned her to them.

Unfortunately, thus far Sam's efforts had led to disappointment.

Early last Season, he'd spoken to his parents about a woman he'd thought to marry. Sam and Miss Appleton shared many of the same interests and seemed to get along well enough in each other's company. When he broached the topic of marriage, however, she admitted to being in love with another man. Sam had been stunned.

Because of that experience, he had not planned to speak openly about Gemma. Now, however, it seemed he'd cornered himself. "I have. Though I do not wish to spur your hopes."

Father waggled the pruning shears at him. "If that smile you wear is any indication, you must have your own."

Was he still smiling? Sam found the answer as he scrubbed a hand over his jaw, taking note of the fissures on either side of his mouth.

Bemused, he shook his head. "You mistake the gesture. This is merely the look of a man who passed a few moments in pleasurable company."

"What do you know of her?"

"Virtually nothing," he said quickly, plucking a pointed leaf from the nearest stem and twirling it between his fingers. Yet his statement earned that singular sharp puff of air from deep in Father's throat that indicated his disbelief. In Sam's youth, that one sound had conditioned him to confess the entire truth of his escapades. *Yes, Father, I was batting rocks into the field*—then that sound—*and I might have been the one who broke the window in the crofter's cottage.*

Apparently, it still worked. "She is somewhat shy but uncommonly clever, and quite honest as well. She wouldn't even dare to deceive a fish."

"And *beautiful?*"

Sam closed his eyes briefly, replaying the moment when she'd surrendered her smile. He'd been thunderstruck. His breath had caught in his throat, and it had seemed as if there was no distance between them. He could see her features as clearly as if she were lying beside him in the grass and waking him from a dream. "Aye. She has the most striking eyes—a forest green imbued with the deepest blue you can imagine."

"Surely there's a bit more to her than a pair of eyes," his father egged, having a merry laugh at him. Then, suddenly, he began to cough, each new convulsion setting off a series of others. The fit went on and on, his shoulders hunching, and beneath the shadow of his hat, his skin turned ashen.

Alarmed, Sam drew closer, setting his arm around his father for support. "Let us sit on the bench, beneath the shade of the arbor. The afternoon has grown too warm."

Yet the truth was more difficult to bear.

A year ago, Father had suffered a heart seizure after being set upon by highwaymen just outside of London. Since then, he suffered from exhaustion, shortness of breath, and an overall frailty that cast an ominous pall over the halls of Dunnock Park.

Shortly following the attack, both Father and Mother moved into the dower cottage, which wasn't necessary since there was ample room in the manor house. But Sam suspected that Father, selflessly, did not want to die in the very bed that his son would occupy. Father even said that his only wish was to see the manor house full of life and Sam happily settled. There was no need to add that he hoped this would happen before it was too late.

Of course, as a healthy man of six and twenty, Sam wanted a wife for his own reasons. But there was no denying that he wanted to honor his father's request as well.

Sitting on the bench, Father began to regain his breath and color. In the cool shade of the arbor, he stripped off his hat and wiped his brow with a handkerchief, wisps of graying hair receding from his hairline. "Tell me more about this girl. Not for me, of course, but for your mother. You know she'll want every detail, including the girl's taste in earbobs. Seems to believe that you can tell a young woman's character from the jewelry she wears."

Sam was no fool and eyed his father shrewdly. "You needn't tell Mother a thing. As I said, there is no cause to put up the bunting. It was only a moment."

When his father merely waited, with his jaw set and his expression bearing a mask of patience to span a hundred years, Sam expelled a breath and gave in. "I could not tell if she wore earbobs with the way her hair framed her face."

He could see it now, the lustrous curls that escaped her chignon to lie against her cheek and neck. One fat tendril had snaked down toward the frilled lace edge of her bodice, inviting his mind to imagine taking her hair down, pin by pin, and then her dress, button by button...

"And what color was her hair—yellow as those marigold petals or dark as the dirt beneath our feet?"

Sam took a steadying breath. "Much darker and shiny too, like that Arabian we once saw at Tattersalls."

"Hmm. It sounds to me as if you noticed a good deal about her." Father might have turned into a fox for the sly grin he gave. "But did you manage to catch her name?"

Gemma. But Sam did not say it aloud. The name and the memory were his to keep. "We were not introduced, as her aunt was on the hill, and they were to depart to the inn at Banfern Glenn."

Father spluttered, pointing in the general direction of the village with his hat. "But Banfern Glenn is only three miles. Why are you not saddling your horse this instant? Bring that dark-haired beauty and her aunt to dinner this evening. Or better yet, have them stay on for your party."

When Sam had gone to London for the Season but failed to bring home a bride, he took the advice of a friend and decided to host a lengthy party, complete with gentlemen and eligible maidens with their chaperones. His guests were set to arrive the day after tomorrow.

"It is not that simple." Certainly, inviting Gemma had entered his mind, but he would like more time to speak with her, to gauge her interests, to know more of her character. And before any of this, he would need an introduction.

"Falling in love with your mother was the simplest thing I've ever done," Father said, leaping ahead a bit. "Marriage ought to start out that way, at least. After all, there's enough work involved along the way, but loving someone should always be the easy part."

"Love and marriage? I've only just met her," Sam said with mild censure to his ever-impulsive father. "Besides, by your own example, I've witnessed that you love someone by knowing her completely."

Father scoffed. "I learn something new about your mother each and every day. Keeps me on my toes, that one." His mouth quirked in a lopsided grin as his gaze drifted to the whitewashed dower cottage. Through the windows of its octagonal solarium, they could glimpse Mother's form sitting at her quilting rack. "I grant you that it is easier when two people are of the same disposition. You cannot expect a violet to climb an arbor, after all. Thankfully, both your mother and I are like these roses, changing and merging as we grow older. There may have been thorns along the way but there was, and is, plenty of beauty. And at the roots, the heart of it all, is what brought us together in the first place."

Sam inhaled slowly, trying to remain patient as he explained his process to Father. Again. "That is all I'm attempting to do—find a woman with whom I'm compatible. This is a serious undertaking and requires careful consideration."

He knew, all too well, what it was like to be mistaken in assessing a young woman's regard for him. He'd even thought to court Juliet, formerly Lady Granworth. Soon enough, however, he'd had found that—similar to Miss Appleton—her heart had been claimed by another as well.

His experience last Season was an irrefutable lesson in caution.

"*Bah.* A rose knows another rose in an instant." Father set his jaw, his lips in a firm line, and looked askance at Sam. "But perhaps you're more like the orchid, with a need to assess the soil and temperature before you bloom. Heaven help us if you find another orchid who is just as skittish."

"Harsh words, considering you've always believed orchids were too fragile and finicky," Sam said, mildly wounded. He was only being careful.

Father patted his forearm but with little sympathy. "That's only because I never had any luck with them. I suppose I'm not patient enough."

An understatement if ever there was one.

Though, ironically, where Sam usually had patience in abundance, today he was sorely lacking. He couldn't wait to see Gemma again.

Yet by her own admission, she was only passing through. Likely not someone who would even be able to stay for a party.

Besides, he was busy with preparations. The guests were arriving the day after next, and of the four young women he'd invited, he hoped one of them might become his bride. Overall, his hands were quite full.

So did it matter that he'd been thunderstruck at the pond, when he'd never felt that way before?

Without conscious thought, as if his body were no longer under the control of his mind, Sam stood, put on his coat, and tugged at the cuffs of his sleeves. Then he heard himself say, "I'm going for a ride."

Apparently, that was his answer.

"There's a good lad." Father stood as well, his pruning tool at the ready near the roses. "A man always needs to present flowers when paying a call on his future—" He stopped at Sam's warning growl, offering a sheepish shrug.

"I'm not paying a call. I just…need to clear my head. That's all."

Besides, if he were to *happen upon* Gemma in Banfern Glenn, he wouldn't give her roses. He'd give her robust, determined blossoms that took root wherever and whenever they pleased.

And he knew just where to find them.

Chapter Three

Looking into the small oval mirror in her room at the inn, Gemma cringed. Her cheeks and the tip of her nose were bright pink from the sun. At the base of her throat, there was a noticeable grayish smear of what could only be a combination of perspiration and road dust. Her hair was a complete disaster of frizzy, windswept curls. Her chignon was no more than a snarled knot, and there appeared to be—oh, *splendid*—a leaf sticking out of the top.

Lovely. Just lovely, she thought with a sneer. Seeing her reflection brought a wholly new dimension to her encounter with Sam. He'd been so warm and engaging that she'd actually thought she'd made quite an impression at the pond. *Yes, as a deranged lunatic on leave from the asylum. A wine-poached-pear slaughterer on the loose.*

Most likely, he'd been unable to look away from the oddity she presented, as if she were under glass in a curiosity shop. Even Berta, her aunt's maid, had looked horrified by the sight of her and asked if she'd taken ill during the picnic. It was clear, however, that she'd really wanted to know if Gemma had taken leave of her senses.

In a way, she had. All the way to Banfern Glenn, which hadn't been too far at all, she felt as if a different person resided in her skin. A young woman who could not stop smiling and sighing wistfully, replaying the scene by the pond in her mind as if the images were painted in a spinning paper lantern, whirling hypnotically around a candle flame.

By the time they'd arrived at the inn, she'd even convinced herself that she might see Sam again. But then the mirror cruelly mocked her.

Squeezing cool water from a square of flannel and into the basin, she wiped away the worst of the grime from her skin. Not seeing him again was for the best, she told herself. After all, it would come to nothing once he learned her surname.

So why did knowing that not lessen her disappointment?

Gemma's morose thoughts were interrupted by the sound of a knock on the door across the hall, where Aunt Edith would sleep. If there hadn't been two rooms available, they would have shared, but Aunt Edith was rather particular about having her own bed and even traveled with a bolster pillow, designed for her to recline without mussing her hair. Knowing that little quirk was one of the things that made Gemma even fonder of her aunt.

"Beg pardon, Your Grace," one of the inn's maids said, "but there's a gentleman here."

Gemma's breath hitched. A gentleman here? But they knew no one in Banfern Glenn. In fact, the only person she'd met was...*Sam.*

"He's inquiring about a young woman and her aunt," the maid continued, "and I wasn't certain what to tell him."

Gemma's heart stalled, and the air left her lungs as if her lacings were suddenly too tight. No. It was impossible. She refused to let her mind take a wild flight of fancy, imagining that the man she'd met by the pond, little more than an hour ago, was now here in this very inn. The mirror agreed, looking even more shocked and doubtful.

But then the door burst open and her aunt's grayish blue eyes danced with such bright joy they were hard to look at. Even in the flurry, not a single strand of her elaborate silvery coiffure dared move out of place. Without hesitation, she rushed to envelop Gemma in a powdery, lavender-scented embrace. "It must be him, my dear. You may shake your head all you like, but it is the only likely conclusion. Clearly, your gentleman from the pond has come to pay a call."

"He is not *my* gentleman," she croaked, unable to catch her breath. "We haven't even been introduced."

Releasing her, Aunt Edith turned to the mobcapped maid waiting in the corridor. "Send the gentleman up, please. We'll be in the parlor in a minute."

"I'm not even dressed! And Berta has gone to the laundress to see if there is anything to be done with my stained muslin." Gemma had barely had time to don a fresh petticoat. And there was still the matter of her hair.

"Never mind all that." Aunt Edith closed the door and pointed to the open trunk. "I know how to button up a dress. Here, take this green-and-white striped frock from the top, as it will be less wrinkled than the others."

Gemma's limbs moved in a blind rush, matching the new, frantic pace of her heart. She pulled the garment over her head and slid her arms into the sleeves before she even put conscious thought into the action. Could it really be him?

"You made quite an impression," Aunt Edith said, placing a pair of green slippers on the floor in front of her. Apparently, she didn't have a single doubt of the identity of their visitor.

Gemma shook her head, not trusting herself to believe it as she wiggled one foot and then the other into the shoes. "Impossible. These terrible curls were clinging to my cheeks, my dress blotched with red wine, not to mention wet from the knee down. *And* I was barefoot."

Her aunt spun her around and began to button the back. "Some men prefer women in a more natural state."

"*Aunt Edith!*" Gemma gasped, laughed, and blushed all at once.

"I did not mean au naturel. Although," she mused, a teasing lilt to her voice, "there are plenty of men who prefer that as well. But then society would fall into chaos, no matters of business would ever conclude, and all because the men would be too preoccupied."

"You are incorrigible." Gemma lifted her eyes to the slanted ceiling of dark wood beams and yellowed plaster overhead.

"A family trait, I'm afraid, so be warned." Her aunt tutted, plucking the leaf from her hair. "Besides, you are now two and twenty, and it is high time you know of these things."

"That women are capable of bringing about the collapse of society? And the only reason it runs at all is because we decide to wear clothes?"

"Precisely." Aunt Edith opened the door and nudged her out through the narrow archway and into the corridor.

But Gemma stopped short, for standing not ten paces from her was none other than Sam. The maid must have forgotten to close the door between the guests' common room and the corridor leading to the chambers.

There he was, bathed in the golden light of the window beside him and staring directly at her. Dressed as he'd been before—though his hair was now charmingly mussed—he was even more handsome than she remembered. Her lungs fluttered again as she struggled for breath, the pulse at her throat leaping like a rabbit.

"Bother it all, I forgot to tie your sash," Aunt Edith said from behind her and busily began tugging at the dark green ribbon. She must not have seen that they had an audience.

Gemma felt her cheeks grow hot. This made the second time she found herself in a state of undress in front of him. Then, as if this realization struck him at the same time, his blue gaze turned warm, roaming down the length of her before he stepped out of view, providing a moment of belated privacy.

Closing her eyes, she tried to calm herself, but the excitement bubbling inside her made it difficult. Worse, she had the startling impulse to rush into the room and fling her arms around Sam's neck. Clearly, this was becoming a problem. In the course of an hour, she'd gone from wanting to embrace a cloud and now a man she hardly knew.

She took a breath, willing her pulse to slow. After all, she would never have lasted a moment in an Egyptian bazaar if she'd approached a *tajir* with any eagerness over bargaining for a brooch or even a handful of dates.

Not only that, but her brief foray into London society had taught her to be cautious in all circumstances. She'd learned quickly that once people heard her name, their true natures were revealed. She'd earned censorious glowers accompanied by whispers, open insults to her character, and even the cut direct.

With that reminder, she suddenly did not want to see what Sam's reaction would be. In the best scenario, he would leave and no longer desire an acquaintance. She hated to imagine the worst.

Another nudge from Aunt Edith drew her attention. "Let us not make him wait too long. Clearly, he is eager to see you again."

Only because he knows nothing about me.

Steeling herself, Gemma walked into the parlor, one footstep on the hardwood floor for every eight beats of her heart. Lifting her gaze slowly, she saw that his tall, brown beaver hat was on the scarred round table in the center of the room. He stood behind it, his shoulders straight and arms behind his back. His camel-colored coat was parted to reveal the green waistcoat that now matched her clothes, but why that made her blush return, she did not know.

Moving around her, Aunt Edith crossed the room without any of the trepidation Gemma felt. "Good day to you, sir. I am pleased to make your—*oh*, but we are already acquainted. You are Viscount Ellery, are you not? If I recall correctly, you attended a party at my nephew's country estate last Christmas."

Ellery? But Gemma knew that title. Her dear friend, Juliet Harwick, the Marchioness of Thayne, had mentioned a desire to introduce her to Lord Ellery on a number of occasions, but they had all come to naught. What a strange coincidence that Gemma should meet him here in Surrey.

He smiled with undisguised pleasure and bowed his head. "Indeed, Your Grace. The Duke of Vale was a gracious host, and I was honored by the invitation. I was also reacquainted with your other nephew, the Earl of Wolford, during that time."

He knew her cousins too? Then surely he would be familiar with her name. At the thought, a renewed sense of dread filled her.

"Then it only seems proper that I acquaint you with my entire family," Aunt Edith said. "Please, allow me to introduce my niece, Miss Gemma Desmond."

Gemma stiffened, waiting for him to recall the number of times her father's name had been in bold ink on every London paper. In the next instant, his smile would surely fade, and he would make a hasty excuse for retreat.

"Miss Desmond," he said, his focus solely on her, his gaze still warm and genial.

She curtsied by rote, stunned by his reaction, or lack thereof. "It is a pleasure to make your acquaintance, Lord Ellery."

Could it be that he did not judge her character as being like her father's? But no, in the past few months she'd learned that such things were impossible. He must have simply forgotten the notorious surname.

Unfortunately, that meant it was left to her or Aunt Edith to inform him. Since her aunt believed that the right man would overlook Albert Desmond's sins in favor of her niece's charms, Gemma knew that the task fell upon her.

While she was mulling over how to begin, he moved his arms from behind his back and presented a bouquet of flowers, astounding her further. Spilling over his hand, the creamy white, pink-tinged petals stood out in sharp contrast against his tanned flesh and somehow made the gesture all the sweeter. She could not imagine such a hand picking flowers. Especially not for her.

All other thoughts vanished. "Woodbines are my favorites."

"Are they?" From the quick lift of his dark golden brows and broader smile, this clearly pleased him. "Then it is fortunate I have so many in bloom at Dunnock Park this time of year. Perhaps you noticed them growing near the willows."

She nodded sheepishly, still hesitant to step forward. "At the time, I did not know it was *your* pond and *your* hill upon which we chose to trespass."

"In our own defense, it was a perfectly situated spot for a picnic," Aunt Edith said without any remorse. She often did exactly as she pleased and would have stopped on his hill even if there were warning notices posted on every tree and rock.

Sam shook his head dismissively. "Fear not, for we gave up the practice of shooting offenders ages ago."

This earned a rare, lilting laugh from Aunt Edith. "It is good you brought some flowers with you as it saves me from stealing my own. Though, since they have been out of water for so long, we dare not even wait for the maid's return to put them in a vase. Therefore, I shall fetch water from the pitcher in my chamber and return presently."

Then, without standing on ceremony, she swept from the room and left Lord Ellery and Gemma quite alone.

"Forgive me," he said, moving closer, casting a brief frown down to the shyly drooping blossoms. "I did not take measures to keep them from wilting or even to tie them together with a ribbon for presentation."

She tilted up her face to study him, noticing that he was tall but not in a looming, threatening manner. There was nothing about him that warned her to keep her distance. Quite the opposite. He possessed an aura of warmth and confidence that emboldened her to reach out.

"The journey has made them all the more beautiful. In fact, I could not imagine a more perfect bundle." The instant Gemma clasped the flowers, a jolt rushed through her. She snatched her hand away. The hot, static shock of her fingers bumping against his was like touching the door latch in the middle of winter. Instinctively, she closed her hand, her flesh tingling. "I—I was not…that is to say…I should be wearing gloves."

"No, indeed, for then the stems would surely cause a stain. It is better this way," he said, his voice hoarse as if he were equally affected. His eyes were darker than before, his irises a bright blue halo surrounding his expanded pupil.

Chiding herself for making him wait, she tried again. Yet with the second attempt, the sensation was even stronger because she was more deliberate in her actions. Curling her fingers around his, the rough graze of his knuckles against her palm sent a series of feverish currents through her, zipping along her limbs, her torso, and then settling in a spot below her navel.

A nervous laugh escaped her. The unbound stems refused to transfer easily from his grasp to hers, and she fumbled the exchange, their fingers tangling, twining together, until she was quite out of breath.

"Gemma," he breathed, the heat of it reaching her lips in a tantalizing sweep. "Tell me you are glad that I have come. If you are not, I will leave at once."

She had to gather her wits. Locked together as they were, with the sweet, heady musk of the flowers rising between them, made her lightheaded. "By your own insistence just now, I *must* tell you that I am glad, for you have given me no other option."

"You're right. I'm being impossibly rude and making a poor impression of my character. I have no excuse other than"— he looked down at the flowers, and beneath the petals, his thumb lightly stroked her flesh—"the perfume of woodbines must affect me strangely. Truthfully, I am far more hesitant by nature."

"As am I," she admitted but tried to remember why. It seemed perfectly natural to have their hands intertwined, to stand close enough to catch the fresh, windblown fragrance of summer sun rising from his clothes and the enticing earthiness beneath it that must surely have been his own intoxicating essence.

He nodded in agreement. "At the pond, your cautious gestures revealed as much, and to your credit. I, however, have been acting like a madman from the first moment."

"Hardly crazed," she said, feeling strangely drowsy, her limbs languid, her eyelids heavy. "The gentleman before me is all kindness."

He shook his head but grinned. "Then I am loath to spoil your good opinion by telling you how close I am to commanding you to attend a village dance this evening."

The sound of a door closing and footsteps in the corridor reminded Gemma that they were not alone. Disentangling her fingers from his, she took a step back toward the hearth, clutching the flowers to her breast and feeling her cheeks grow hot again. "Why not simply ask?"

"Because a plea leaves too much to chance, when I would rather have certainty before I go."

She shook her head. "But you only just arrived."

"Yes, as I keep reminding myself. But that does not seem to slow this inexplicable desire to rush forward from introduction to—" He stopped, his tone possessing an undercurrent of heat that made him sound quite rakish. Then, darting a glance to the doorway, he retreated as well, picked up his hat, and held it before him.

"You are not leaving already, Lord Ellery?" Aunt Edith said, setting a buttery yellow earthenware cup, filled with water, in the center of the table. "I should ring for a tray to give you a proper welcome."

"Thank you, ma'am, but having already arrived without warning, I would only add to my crimes by overstaying. I know what it is like to travel a distance and find myself in need of a bed—" His words broke, and he cleared his throat. Then, hastily, he bowed, the gesture stilted as if he were suffering a malady of some sort. "Or *rest*, rather."

Aunt Edith clucked her tongue. "For a young gentleman who was so eager only moments ago, I find myself curious at this abrupt departure."

Gemma wondered as well, and felt as if this encounter was slipping out of her grasp too quickly. Had he tired of her company so quickly?

He shrugged, chagrined. "I confess that I was just informing Miss Desmond of a village dance this evening in the hall next door. If you have no other engagements, I would be honored to escort you both."

When his fervid gaze drifted to her, Gemma could not stop the ebullient feeling strumming through her veins.

Her aunt turned, a cheeky smile on her lips as she took the flowers from her grasp and began arranging them in the cup. "Gemma, dear, in the forty minutes we have been in Banfern Glenn, have we already accepted an invitation from a gentleman bearing your favorite flowers?"

Gemma smiled too. "I seem to recall turning all the others away."

Expecting Sam to laugh and wanting to hear that rich, effortless sound again, she was surprised by the lack of amusement in his expression. His cordial smile still curved his lips, but his eyes were searching and serious. In that flash of an instant, she sensed that this meeting was no mere lark for him. It could even be that he genuinely liked her, perhaps as much as she already liked him.

As her heart soared at the notion, reality brought it crashing down. He still didn't know who she was.

It was time to tell him the truth. All of it. Even at the risk of never seeing him again.

"There have been no other gentlemen callers." She swallowed to soothe away the tremble from her voice. "Not today and likely not ever. The reason is because—"

"Because Gemma was new to London," Aunt Edith hastily interrupted, "and did not participate in the Season. Therefore, she did not have the opportunity to earn the admiration of other gentlemen who might have called on her."

Sam visibly relaxed, the stiffness leaving his posture, his grin even warmer than before. "Then it is to my own good fortune. Only a fool would not see this as an advantage. So until later, I bid you both a good day."

Then, without lingering a moment longer, he inclined his head and summarily departed.

"Good day." Gemma was left to stare after him as he ducked his head through the doorway.

Once they were alone, Aunt Edith clapped her hands together. "That could not have gone any better. I daresay he will arrive early this evening in order to spend more time in your company."

Gemma frowned, a wave of guilt washing over her. "I should have told him about my father."

"No, you should not have," her aunt replied with a sternness she usually saved for Cousin North and Cousin Liam. "Give him the chance to know you, to like you even more than he already does."

"Do you think he likes me?" Of course, Gemma had already surmised the answer, but she took a guilty moment to savor the light fluttering feeling it caused inside her.

"There is no mistaking it. In fact, if I'd have stayed out of the room a second longer, he might have tried to kiss you."

"Surely not." But Gemma felt her cheeks grow hot beneath her aunt's mirthful scrutiny. "Besides, I wouldn't have let him. I have more sense than that."

Aunt Edith laughed. "If the pair of you were starving and someone laid a seven-course meal on the table, you wouldn't have noticed. I was young once too and felt the same way when I met my husband."

The words were enough to jolt Gemma into reality again. She walked to the window and stared down at the narrow cobblestone lane. "Viscount Ellery will not become my husband. Once he learns who my father is, he will feel foolish for even making my acquaintance."

"You judge him, and yourself, too harshly. I know his parents, and they are just as kind and courteous as he is."

"Which only makes it worse," Gemma said, admitting a painful truth. The reason she needed a husband was to change her name into something more palatable to society. That was the only way she could escape the censure that had befallen everyone she cherished. "Though you have tried to shield me from the knowledge, I know how often you have been snubbed because your niece with the *bad blood* resides beneath your roof. I have also seen it happen with my cousins and their wives. North and Ivy, and Liam and Adeline, may not care about what the gossips say, but I do."

One would think that with a duke and an earl in the family, their reputations would not exist on tenterhooks. However, there were still members of the *ton* who objected to North's succession to the dukedom, calling his mother's lineage into question. And there were even those who thought Liam was nothing more than a rake and a spendthrift.

"Given enough time, all will be forgotten."

"Not *all*. My father nearly murdered Adeline by trying to send her to the bottom of the Thames. And even if society could forget about that, the many people he swindled and made laughingstocks of never will, as long I hold the name of Desmond." Gemma's gaze drifted over her shoulder to the flowers, and guilt washed over her. "When it was clear that Lord Ellery did not know who I was, I should have told him everything without delay. By not doing so, I have turned into a common schemer."

"Hardly," Aunt Edith scoffed. "I daresay you were taken off guard by discovering the one stranger who didn't instantly cast your worth into the same pit as your father's. In that you can be forgiven, surely."

Hmm... Gemma had her doubts. "Regardless, I cannot use Viscount Ellery's unwitting affability to suit my own purpose."

"You could always ask him," Aunt Edith said, as if it were a simple matter.

Her aunt's pragmatism drew a sardonic laugh from her. Gemma faced the empty doorway and curtsied, pretending to see him there. "Viscount Ellery, if you would be kind enough to allow me to share your name for a few decades, that would be splendid. A nice, abundantly handsome gentleman such as yourself surely has no other options than to marry a young woman out of pity."

"Or you could marry for love instead."

Gemma rolled her eyes. "Since I do not believe a new fissure has split apart the earth's crust, spewing forth a mountain of new possibilities for my life, I'm going to assume you've taken too much sun this afternoon. And perhaps I have too. Otherwise, I never would have agreed to attend the dance. What *was* I thinking?"

"I should hope you were thinking that you might enjoy yourself. That is the purpose of our holiday, after all," Aunt

Edith said, apparently forgetting that she'd spoken of little else than Gemma's upcoming Season and catching a husband since they'd left London. "Do not fret over the future or place any urgent expectations on a mere dance."

Gemma eyed her aunt skeptically. "You're one to talk. No doubt, in the space of this conversation, you've decided on the amount of lace you'd like for my wedding gown and planned my honeymoon trip to Bath."

"Which proves how little you know me, my dear. I was thinking of *ruffles* and *Italy*, of course." Aunt Edith flashed her pearly teeth, her eyes brightening. "Oh, and should you and Lord Ellery have a daughter, the name Edith Charlotte has a nice ring to it. Wouldn't you agree?"

CHAPTER FOUR

"What a slugabed you've been this morning," Aunt Edith scolded the following day, but with an undercurrent of amusement as Gemma leaned down to buss her cheek.

In the upstairs parlor, Gemma slipped into a chair and arranged her blue muslin skirts. On the small table before her, a selection of scones, sliced meats, and coddled eggs awaited. She was famished and wanted to devour everything in sight. "Forgive me. I know we planned to go exploring today. Yet for some reason, I could not awaken. I slept so soundly that I did not even hear Berta come into my room to lay out this dress for me."

"Hmm...I wonder if, perhaps, we should put the blame on Lord Ellery. Clearly, he overexerted you with all that dancing last night, and I daresay that your face was as pink as Mrs. Selby's punch."

"He did nothing of the sort," Gemma said in Sam's defense. Trying to tuck the perfect memories from last night away for safekeeping, she calmly laid a serviette over her lap. "My face was pinkened from too much sun. That is all."

Gemma did her best to ignore her aunt's pleased grin and her own inner palpitations. Yet the memory of the dance was so fresh that she could still feel the warm press of Sam's hand, the brush of his limbs against hers, and the lingering gazes that sent a cascade of tingles through her entire body. Gooseflesh rose on her arms as if every moment had been embedded into her skin and she would carry them with her always.

She hadn't wanted the night to end. By all appearances, neither had he.

He'd danced two full sets with her and might have danced a third, if not for the rule that stated a gentleman could not dance three sets without declaring his intentions. Nevertheless, after the second set, he'd then invited her to join him in the courtyard—within full view of Aunt Edith, of course. And there, seated side by side on a low stone wall, they'd drunk the delicious punch that the innkeeper's wife made and talked about how lovely the day had been, as if they both wanted to live it over and over again.

Aunt Edith lifted the teapot and poured a cup for Gemma. "I never realized how many teeth you possessed until I saw you twirling around the assembly room on Lord Ellery's arm."

"Is that your sly way of saying you caught me smiling at my dance partner? How scandalous."

"My dear, there are smiles, and then there are…*smiles*," she said with a wealth of meaning and a lift of her penciled brows.

Gemma carefully stirred honey into her tea. "What I did was allow myself a measure of enjoyment, knowing full well that was my first and last country dance in Banfern Glenn. After all, you remembered quite late to tell me that you'd sent a missive to Lady Donrolin the instant we arrived at the inn yesterday."

A most distressing truth.

When she'd told Gemma the news, Aunt Edith had been certain that her friend would send for them straightaway. In fact, they'd journeyed to Surrey because of Lady Donrolin's unflappable eagerness to see Edith.

So many other *supposed* friends had cast her aside because she had not distanced herself from Albert Desmond's daughter.

Aunt Edith had been looking forward to this visit for some time. And, of course, Gemma was happy it would come to pass. She was not in the least bit disappointed that they were to leave Banfern Glenn just when it had become the most interesting place in the world. Not at all.

Gemma swallowed, feeling the beginnings of a dull ache in the center of her chest. It sat there, pressing heavily upon her, as if she were beneath the collection of robust atlases in Cousin North's library. Her appetite suddenly dimmed.

Even though Lady Donrolin's estate was also in Surrey and would likely be beautiful, Gemma doubted it had a pond surrounded by woodbine and a perfectly situated picnic hill. More important, it did not house a gentleman with clear blue eyes and an easy laugh.

"It doesn't necessarily have to be our last day in Banfern Glenn," Aunt Edith said offhandedly as she added a dollop of clotted cream to her scone. Yet her words were edged with the unmistakable weight of disappointment, pulling all the syllables downward.

Gemma had always possessed an unconscious ability to read a person's gestures or hear the subtle shifts in a voice.

And in the past months, she had become all too familiar with that particular tone.

Alert at once, Gemma saw the faint spider web of wrinkles around Aunt Edith's mouth, her lips pressed into a forced smile that did not reach her eyes.

Something had happened. Looking for the answer, Gemma noticed the folded blue-tinted paper tucked beneath the edge of her aunt's plate. "Is that a missive from Lady Donrolin?"

Aunt Edith followed Gemma's gaze. "It is. And happy news for us, I should think. Our schedule is free once again, giving us the opportunity to scamper about the countryside at will."

"Might I read it?" Gemma asked, sensing there was more than *happy news*.

Aunt Edith's pasted smile slipped. She lowered her spoon, the neck settling against the rim of the plate with an ominous *clack*. "Dearest, the only good this letter serves is to keep my plate from wobbling on an uneven table."

"Surely it can be no worse than the others I've read."

Seeing her determination, Aunt Edith offered a wary nod.

Gemma withdrew the folded missive, expecting it to be like the others and full of excuses. An illness in the family, perhaps? A spontaneous holiday that would keep them away for an indeterminate amount of time? Or even having all the guest chambers redecorated at the once? Surprisingly, there had been two idiotic ninnies who'd used that excuse.

But none of those reasons was present here. Lady Donrolin was far more direct.

In unapologetic, decisive script, she cited that since her daughters were preparing for next Season in London, and given the fact that "a certain Miss Desmond" was Edith's traveling companion, she could "no longer afford the association." She also included a list of nunneries in France, known to accept the "less desirable" debutante.

How helpful.

"I see." Gemma felt every vertebra of her back stiffen. She folded the missive and replaced it, none too gently, beneath Aunt Edith's plate.

All Gemma had wanted when she returned to London was a normal, quiet life. She didn't want to cause a scandal wherever she went. Nor did she want to be the topic of conversation or have all of her actions dissected and examined for traces of evil. She just wanted to be happy and spend time with the family she'd been apart from for too long.

Aunt Edith's diminished social standing only worsened the remorse Gemma felt. Because of it, she'd vowed to do anything to ensure her aunt's happiness. Even marry in order to change her name.

"So what's it to be then?" Aunt Edith dusted her hands together. "Shall we continue our nomadic holiday? Or, if you prefer, we could return to North and Ivy's country house and await the arrival of the baby. After all, eight weeks can go by in a blink. At least some of the time, I'm sure."

There was no mistaking the faint red lines in her aunt's eyes, or the trace of shimmering liquid along the rim of her lower lid. So Gemma weighed their options but with her aunt's happiness foremost in her mind.

However, before she could answer, a maid opened the outer door and dipped into a curtsy. "Lord Ellery, Your Grace."

Gemma's heart stalled in her throat. She didn't even have time to recover before Sam swept into the room.

His gaze fixed on her instantly. Even from the distance of four or more steps, she could see the penumbra of bright blue around his dark pupils. Being the sole focus of his attention, she felt hot, as if her body were submerged in this cup of tea, her blood flowing like hot honey through her veins. She could still feel him dancing with her, the press of his hand against the curve of her back...

He removed his hat and bowed. "Your Grace. Miss Desmond. I pray you will forgive my bold intrusion this morning."

Since Gemma couldn't seem to form any words or manage one full breath, she was thankful that Aunt Edith spoke. "You are more than welcome, Lord Ellery. We were just remarking on what a fine time we had last evening, for which we have you to thank."

"I was more than delighted to be of service," he said, stepping further into the room, looking from Aunt Edith to Gemma. "In fact, that is the reason for my call yet again. I remembered from our conversation in the courtyard that you had no fixed plans for today."

Had she revealed that last night? Thinking back, Gemma recalled saying quite a lot of things, and none of them what she should have said. She'd taken Aunt Edith's advice and kept the truth of her father from their conversation. Instead, she'd given in to an evening of enjoyment, knowing how fleeting it was meant to be.

Now, however, it seemed she was faced with another opportunity to confess the truth. And it would guarantee that she would not see Sam again. The pleasant warmth she felt evaporated like steam, leaving her cold.

"I am all eagerness to learn of your plan, Lord Ellery," Aunt Edith said, her tone lifting upward in delight.

Sam looked directly at Gemma. "I thought you might find it amenable to take a tour of the countryside."

"A heaven-sent invitation." Aunt Edith clasped her hands over her heart and turned her beaming face to Gemma. "What do you think, my dear? Shall we allow ourselves one more day of utter enjoyment?"

One more day. The words were as exhilarating as they were heartbreaking.

Gemma knew she should refuse. Keeping this secret from him made her all the more greedy and selfish. Yet after the letter from Lady Donrolin, and being the cause of another severed relationship for Aunt Edith, how could Gemma add to her disappointment?

One more day, Gemma thought. *One more day and then no more.*

Decided, and before she lost her nerve, Gemma nodded.

"**W**hat a splendid afternoon, Lord Ellery," the Dowager Duchess of Vale said with a contented exhale, her parasol twirling at her shoulder as she faced their view of the vast rolling hills from their picturesque spot on Leith Hill. "How could you have known that my niece and I required this outing to lift us out of our doldrums?"

Sam paused in the midst of packing up the picnic basket, his gaze on Gemma, who was on the other side of it, doing the same. "Until this moment, I had not known you'd needed rescuing."

He'd sensed nothing amiss during these past hours. They'd both seemed to greet the outing with the same fervor he felt, sharing lively conversation that lacked any of the awkwardness often present with a new acquaintanceship. It was comfortable and without the fuss of formality. At least, that's what he'd assumed until now.

"It is nothing," Gemma said quickly, fitting both hands around the slender jar of punch he'd procured from Mrs. Selby as if her answer were trapped inside. She hesitated, her pupils receding to tiny points, making the green-blue of her irises look stark. Then, she lifted one delicate shoulder in a shrug. "Only that our future plans went...awry."

Standing in the middle of the clearing, the dowager duchess offered a discontented huff but did not elaborate on the matter.

Curious, he looked again to Gemma, only to find her fumbling with the swollen cork stopper and getting the tip of her glove caught. He didn't like the awkwardness that had suddenly risen up between them.

"I'm sorry about your plans," he said simply, extending his hand in a silent request for the jar. When she complied, he settled his hand gently over hers and felt the barest tremble rush through her. He wanted to ease the worry he saw in her shielded gaze, and he wanted to know what had *gone awry*. Yet he had the sense that she did not want to speak about the subject. If possible, Gemma seemed even more hesitant in nature and cautious than he was.

Then, Gemma appeared to recover herself. The somberness he thought he'd witnessed slipped away from the tipped corners of her bow-shaped mouth, and the virescent shade of her eyes deepened once more. It must have been an aberration.

"You are kind to say so," she said quietly, "but my aunt and I are determined to continue our nomadic holiday and find enjoyment enough that all else is forgotten."

There, he thought, watching her closely. Did a tinge of sadness just cross her expression? "Is there something you wish to forget?"

Her gaze darted up to his and widened slightly in surprise as if she'd revealed something that she hadn't intended to do. He did his best to study every nuance of her expression, wanting to know everything about her. Already, he was prepared to slay whatever beast dared to make her feel anything but joy. The world needed the sound of her laugh and the sight of her smiles.

She expelled a weighty sigh that settled in the air between them. "Let us not speak of wishes. Instead, tell us of Surrey and of all the places we must visit."

The last thing he wanted was to sour her to his company by pressuring her and ignoring her reluctance to speak on this topic. So instead, he thought of this as an opportunity to ease into knowing her better.

"I have a better suggestion," he said, the ready words spilling from his lips. Closing the lid on the basket, he clapped his hands together and chafed them with eagerness. "There is to be a lengthy party in a house not far from here. If you and your aunt were to attend, it promises to fulfill all of your expectations for enjoyment."

"Oh, we are quite in need of enjoyment." The dowager duchess tilted her parasol and turned to him, her smile and brows lifted in expectation. A good sign, indeed.

Gemma, however, eyed him with unquestionable skepticism. "By chance, is this party at Dunnock Park?"

"Do you know the place?" He feigned shock and earned a smirk in return. "I can see that you hold doubts, but in truth, there will be three gentlemen and four young ladies with their chaperones arriving at my home tomorrow."

He stood and automatically breached the distance between them and settled his hand beneath her elbow, as if he'd been doing so for years. Normally, he was not so forward and should apologize. Yet when her delicate hand briefly squeezed his forearm as she straightened, it pleased him to imagine that she did not mind. The hardest part was letting her go.

Gemma smoothed her skirts and looked askance at him. "And adding yourself to the list makes for a convenient number for a party—a gentleman for each lady."

At her summation, the dowager duchess made a tsking sound, and he felt as if he might have lost a bit of headway.

He rallied quickly, however, adding a thoughtful nod for good measure. "True, but that is not to say that the addition of another young lady *and* her aunt would disturb the balance."

"How could it not?" Gemma shook her head, and when she pursed her lips, the bottom one looked so plump—so enthrallingly soft—that it begged to be kissed…

He tore his gaze away and shook his head. Better not give in to distraction. This was too important.

"At parties such as these," he continued, "it is often that one guest does not wish to participate in certain activities, so it is always beneficial to have another on hand."

"You require a spare?" Gemma issued an amused scoff and looked over her shoulder to her aunt.

"It is not entirely unheard of," the dowager duchess said, offering a smile of apparent encouragement to Sam.

Somehow, he managed to hold back his own grin as he nodded. "In fact, I usually keep one in the attic for such occasions. But with the summer being so hot, and the windows left open in the evenings…well, the bats have become a problem, chasing off my usual spare guest. So you see, I absolutely must invite your parasol-wielding aunt. Of course, you're welcome to attend as well."

Gemma smiled fully at him, her captivating eyes glinting as her laughter lit up the hill, brightening even the shady portions beneath the leafy canopy. *Yes*, he thought again, the world—his world—needed more of this. More of her.

Gone was the mere desire to have her attend his party. Now, he was quite determined to make it happen.

"I can see that I never should have told you that story." She pressed her fingertips to her lips and turned to the dowager duchess. "I'm sorry, Aunt Edith, but you will be in high demand as a *spare* at all house parties."

The dowager duchess snickered quietly and closed her parasol. "It took the pair of us to capture the last one, so of course I will drag you with me. You have revealed our secret skill, and now we shall have no peace."

"Oh, but it is peaceful at Dunnock Park," Sam offered, using any advantage he could. "Most mornings you can hear flower petals open; in the afternoons, the whisper of a breeze through the surrounding trees; and each evening, a cricket serenade."

"It sounds idyllic," Gemma said dreamily, as if on the verge of accepting. Then—*hang it all*—she shook her head. "But we cannot attend."

"Whyever not?"

"Because"—she swallowed—"because you have invited your friends, of whom we know none."

A paltry excuse. Why did it seem as if there was more to her reason than what she let on? "I do consider the gentlemen friends of mine. The ladies, however, I do not know as well."

Gemma included. But he planned to remedy that.

"But why would you invite ladies with whom you share little—" She hesitated, her delicate dark brows lifting with curiosity and then lowering in understanding. "Ah. You mean to further an acquaintance with them. Perhaps even…for the purpose of marriage?"

A day ago, he would have agreed with her quick supposition. After all, he wanted to gain a sense of certainty about the women under consideration. Now, however, he couldn't seem to recall a single one of them *or* the reason he'd extended the invitations.

"I believe the three of us may have a mutual friend. Juliet, Lady Granworth—or rather, Lady Thayne, now that she is remarried," he clarified and paused for Gemma's and the dowager duchess's nods. "It was her suggestion that a party would aid in my decision."

"Juliet is full of clever ideas," the dowager duchess interjected. "Both she and Lord Thayne are touring libraries all across the continent for their honeymoon. I have never heard of such an original idea, but it suits the two of them quite well. It is always nice when young people find their counterparts."

Gemma snapped a hard gaze to her aunt in clear warning.

Sam laughed at the dowager duchess's blatant inference. "Ma'am, I do believe that you would get along famously with my parents." The only difference was that Father would have mentioned *marriage* and *Miss Desmond* directly.

When Gemma cast Sam an apologetic look, a fresh blush on her cheeks, they shared a look of commiseration. The sardonic shake of his head must have eased her mind because she smiled in return.

"And I would look forward to renewing the acquaintance… *if* given the chance." The dowager duchess lifted her shoulders in a shrug and stepped toward them. "However, I shall leave that decision to Gemma. In the meantime, I should like to climb the rest of the way toward Prospect House. The tower is simply stunning in the sunlight. From here, the pale shimmer of color makes it appear as if it is made of velum instead of stone, and so I must see it up close before it can blow away. Yet before I go"—she reached into an unseen pocket in her lavender walking costume and withdrew a green velvet pouch, tied with a braided gold cord—"I want to give my favorite niece a small token to mark this most splendid day forever in her memory, as it will surely be in mine."

"Aunt Edith, what have you done?" Gemma chided fondly.

Then the dowager duchess glanced at Sam. "Lord Ellery, I hope you will pardon this level of familiarity I am employing, but I admit I feel quite at my leisure to do whatever I please in your presence."

Gemma cleared her throat and pressed her lips together, as if to keep from smiling, but the phantom of one revealed itself in the lift of her cheeks.

"You do me a great honor, ma'am." Sam inclined his head. He felt a measure of contented relief to know that Gemma's aunt enjoyed his company. In his way of thinking, that won half the battle ahead of him.

Gemma took hold of the pouch, her hesitation marked in the sluggish movements to untie the knot. She even glanced at him apologetically. "This is unpardonably rude."

"Only if you keep us waiting," the dowager duchess said with impatience.

Gemma issued a breathy sound that was surely half exasperation. Yet when she finally managed the knot and peered inside, she gasped.

"Oh, Aunt Edith," she whispered, drawing out a slender strand of coral. "It's beautiful and just like the one in my mother's portrait."

A startled laugh escaped the dowager duchess as Gemma suddenly embraced her. Then her expression turned wistful with a touch of melancholy, giving Sam the understanding that Gemma's mother was gone. He imagined that was the reason she hadn't mentioned her parents. Thus far, she kept her conversation centered on the here and now and observations on whatever was around them. There was still so much he did not know about her.

"The clasp on this is quite tricky, with a hook and a bronze shell to cover it," the dowager duchess said. "I daresay, we will require Lord Ellery's assistance in managing it this first time. That is"—her glistening, pale gaze alighted on Sam—"if he is amenable."

Gemma straightened and stepped out of her aunt's embrace. She shook her head. "That isn't—"

"Yes, of course," he said in the same instant.

"Good. Then it's all settled." The dowager duchess dabbed her eyes with a lace handkerchief and took hold of her parasol as if it were a walking stick, pressing the tip into the grass at her feet. "And now for my walk. I'm certain you will be along presently?"

Sam nodded and then was left very much alone with Gemma. The Dowager Duchess of Vale was quickly becoming one of his favorite people.

Gemma watched her aunt depart and then shyly slid her gaze to him. "You do not have to, you know. I can manage."

"And risk your aunt hunting me down with that vicious parasol of hers? Never." He stepped closer, his pulse thrumming at the mere thought of touching her.

She smiled and held the necklace in her palm, offering it to him. He wasted no time in fitting his hand over hers. The cool hardness of the polished coral beads against his flesh stood out in contrast to the softness of the kid leather. All the same, he would prefer to feel her skin against his. Yet through the thin layer of her glove, there was no mistaking the reflexive hitch of her fingers as they curled into his palm. Was she feeling it too, this inexplicable need to touch him as much as he needed to touch her?

Because of his inability to gauge a woman's interest with complete certainty, he could only guess the answer. And hope.

When she faced away from him, he worked the clasp free and lifted the two ends of the necklace over her head, resting it against the base of her throat. It was a warm day, even here in the shade, but standing this close caused the temperature to blaze. He drew in a steadying breath, thick with the sweet scent of her skin and the intoxicating musk of her perspiration. With her hair gathered up in a twist at her crown, the nape of her neck was exposed and adorned with wispy dark curls.

Not wanting any to tangle in the clasp, he brushed the silken hairs aside. Her skin responded instantly, pebbling in gooseflesh, and her breath quickened. Witnessing her sensitivity to his touch sent a heavy pulse of arousal through him. He'd been battling it all day. It was more than the simple fact that he found her attractive. There were scores of pretty women in London, and a few of them attending his party. But standing beside them, talking to them, or even dancing with any of them had not felt half as good as it had with Gemma. She possessed a vibrancy that captivated him and seemed to fill him when he was near. How could he resist wanting to spend every possible moment with her?

And that was the crux of his problem. He could only spend time with her if she chose to attend his party.

He exhaled, inadvertently parting her curls with his breath, and she shivered. Oh, how he wanted to press his lips there, to taste her flesh. It took a feat of willpower to focus on his task. Then as one more act of torture, as he fastened the clasp, one curl wound itself around his fingertip in a soft clench that sent a corresponding sensation behind the fall of his breeches.

"There," he said at last, his voice hoarse as he took a step back. He wondered how he'd survived.

She was slow to turn and face him, and he was thankful for it because the effect from touching her was quite evident. So he bent to take the handles of the picnic basket and held it awkwardly in front of him.

"Thank you," she said, her face flushed, her fingers skating over the coral strand.

Sam adjusted his hold on the basket as they began their climb up the hill. "My pleasure."

"I hope the clasp was not difficult."

He was about to tell her that it was easy but then inspiration struck. "Exceedingly so. In fact, it may take up to a fortnight before the mechanism can be fastened with ease. I would not be a gentleman if I did not offer my assistance, though our close proximity would be required. Coincidentally, I'm hosting a house party…"

"You don't say."

"I believe it is in your best interest to accept my invitation."

She glanced over her shoulder at him, one corner of her mouth curling wryly. "And all because of my necklace?"

"Well, that *and* your enjoyment. I can guarantee it. I've planned picnics and outings on horseback, lawn billiards, and so much more." He was doing all he could to make Dunnock Park irresistible.

"Hmm. But what if you have a guest who simply desires to sit by the pond and sketch or read a book?"

"Then I am happy to say that Dunnock Park hosts many wonders worthy of ink and paper, not to mention a fine library. I confess, however, that most of the books are more about history, horticulture, and agriculture." Even so, he was quite proud of his collection and found himself spending many an hour happily ensconced in the past, but from the comfort of a chair by the fire. All he wanted was to find someone who would enjoy sitting beside him. "Though I recently acquired several novels for this party as well."

He stopped to step over a fallen oak that blocked their path. Setting down the basket, he offered his hand to her.

"I hope you are not suggesting that women only read novels." She tsked, chiding him playfully as she stepped up on the low end of the tree. Then, releasing him, she set her arms wide and proceeded to follow the trunk to the spindly branches that lay ahead. "Some of us are quite enthralled by reading about ancient civilizations as well as various varieties of flora and fauna. I'll have you know that I routinely engage in debates with my cousin Liam over certain artifacts in his collection and the functions they might have performed. Additionally, I have plucked a variety of leaves from the garden and studied them beneath the lenses of my cousin North's microscope. I find it all fascinating and have spent many a night poring over books in his library and—why are you smiling at me that way?"

He might have fallen in love with her right then and there. It was difficult to tell because his heart was clamoring too loudly within in chest, twirling noisemakers and setting off fireworks. "Because I...I must insist you attend the party. Your merriment is at stake."

"Sam," she said with a short laugh, not knowing what calamitous things hearing his name on her lips did to his heart and lungs. "As I said before, I would know none of your friends."

"What better way to know them?"

Her expression—the wry tilt of her mouth, the glint in her eyes—was caught somewhere between exasperation and amusement. "I fear that whatever answer I give, you will only declare it as a new opportunity to convince me."

He stroked his chin in a show of appearing thoughtful. "Hmm…possibly true. You may as well give in now. I shall send a carriage for you in the morning."

Her hands fell to her hips once again, the action drawing the muslin taut over the perfection of her breasts. "You speak as if I have already given my consent."

"Aye, you have." Sam grinned up at her as he reached up to assist her to the ground. Slipping through her bent arms, his hands settled at her waist. "I can see the future, Miss Desmond."

"Ah," she said, breathless, her face bright with excitement as she laid her hands on his shoulders. "That must have been what you were doing at the pond yesterday—divining the future with your friend, Mr. Pike."

He stayed there, as they were, for a moment longer, knowing that when he lowered her to the ground he would have to release her. "I should like to hear your consent all the same."

She held his gaze and something—he wasn't certain what—passed between them. Then, after a moment, she nodded. "Very well."

Elated, he lifted her from the log and swung her around in a half circle before he set her down on her feet. Then he winked. "Mr. Pike knew it all along."

CHAPTER FIVE

From the carriage window, Gemma looked out at the sprawling brick manor that was Dunnock Park and felt a tight, guilty churning in her stomach. She should not be here. Today was the day of Lord Ellery's party, and her presence could ruin everything for him.

Across from her on the green velvet seat, Aunt Edith exhaled a contented sigh. "'Tis a fine house, is it not?"

Gemma nodded, believing the house to be perfectly situated. She loved the towering shade trees flanking either side and the pale stone surrounding the broad doorway and mullioned windows. Additionally, the flower boxes beneath the windows of the east and west wings gave the façade such a bright cheerfulness that she was almost eager to see inside.

If it weren't for guilt, she might have allowed herself to be excited.

"And what a surprise that we should be here at all"—Aunt Edith paused long enough to tsk—"with your determination to refuse Lord Ellery's invitation."

Gemma wondered where her resolve had gone. She knew that nothing could come of their association. However, instead of confessing the reasons she could not attend, she'd accepted his invitation.

What had she been thinking?

Finding a loose thread on the side of her lace mitts, she began to pick at it. "I do not know quite how it happened."

Aunt Edith's penciled brows lifted as a pleased-as-punch grin stole over her lips. "I, for one, am glad of it. We were fortunate he called yesterday to rescue us from our spoiled plans. He did a fair job of lifting our spirits after…well, we needn't speak about it again."

Neither of them wanted to talk about Lady Donrolin's missive.

Gemma nodded absently. She should have known that spending the day with Sam would turn out in the end. She should have known that his charm and engaging personality made him…irresistible. He often caught her unawares with something to make her smile or laugh, when she was typically more guarded. For most of her life, she'd had to be.

It was an exhausting way to live, always shielding herself from others. But with Sam, it was different. She wasn't entirely sure she could hide herself from him. A terrifying truth.

"I still don't know what came over me. Though I suspect he orchestrated the entire day in order to whittle down my reserves."

Of all the travels she'd had in her life, and of all the exotic and not-so-exotic places she'd been, spending the afternoon on Leith Hill had been the best day of her life by far. And she feared it was not because of the fine view of the towering Prospect House but because of one particular companion.

Aunt Edith sniffed with censure. "A well-sprung open carriage on fine roads, the weather being neither too hot nor too cold, trees and rolling hills as far as the eye can see, a sumptuous basket laden with succulent fruits, decadent cheeses, pastries, breads, and those delightful meringues—*heavens yes*, I can see why you might despise him for that."

"Don't you see? It was too wonderful," she said in dismay. A full day later and she still felt her pulse quicken at the memory of his fitting the clasp of her necklace, his breath stirring the downy hairs curling against her nape, his bare fingertips grazing her flesh.

Gemma's exhale came out in a shudder, and she quickly bit down on the corner of her lip. Wanting to hide the fact that flames were surely rising from her cheeks, she turned to look out the carriage window once more. "He made me forget…things."

Namely, that the presence of Albert Desmond's daughter would likely spoil his grand party. Perhaps they should turn the carriage around before it was too late.

Yet in that same instant, the front door of the manor opened. As if he'd been watching for their carriage, Sam stepped out and onto the stone path, with that brilliant, easy smile on his lips. When he waved, her heart floated upward, lodging at the base of her throat.

Yesterday, he'd made it impossible to allow her mind to veer to any unpleasantness. Likely, that had been the reason why—when he'd settled his hands around her waist to assist her from the fallen tree—she'd given in to impulse and accepted his invitation to his party.

His sublime expression had made her want to freeze that moment in time and stay there forever, just gazing down at him and feeling the way the moon must feel when it gazes down at the earth—bright and blissfully happy. And when he'd winked and stated that Mr. Pike had known the outcome all along, she'd had the most startling urge to kiss him.

First an urge to fling her arms around him and then to kiss him? These impulses were dangerous, indeed. Thankfully, they'd shocked her enough to jolt her back to her senses.

Yet she feared the damage was done all the same. Since then, she hadn't been able to stop wanting to do both.

"I need to tell Lord Ellery the whole truth before I begin to…" Gemma's frantic whisper trailed off as she met her aunt's wistful gaze.

"To care for him?" In receiving a nod, Aunt Edith reached out and patted Gemma's hand. "I'm fairly certain it's too late for that."

"No. It cannot be," she said quickly. "I've learned to be cynical and untrusting when it comes to meeting people." A lesson taught to her most recently at her first, and only, London ball.

Lord Markham had been the one to teach her. He'd lured her onto the terrace at Lady Simpkin's ball, alone, and under the guise of friendly conversation. Yet the fiend had actually expected a tryst.

She'd been fortunate that Juliet had arrived in time to save her from his advances. Even so, that had not stopped his spiteful words. *"She has no future in society, no fortune, and nothing to appeal to a man with serious pursuits. And most of all, she comes from bad blood. There is no man who would willingly choose her to become his wife. At least I am offering her a chance to become something other than a shriveled-up spinster."*

Whatever hope she'd had of marrying for love had died that day. It was quite clear that no decent man would have her. And after living her life surrounded by thieves and scoundrels, Gemma knew she only wanted to marry a good, decent man. But she would have to settle for any man willing to share his name.

"Unflappable cynicism tends to lock the doors that guard one's heart," Aunt Edith said softly, squeezing her hand. "I hope you left a window open for our Lord Ellery."

Gemma was afraid of that very possibility.

Sam spent the entire morning pacing the foyer floor, peering through the windows, and listening for the first sounds of Gemma's carriage. Mr. Fentum, his butler, likely thought he'd gone mad but had been good enough not to say a word.

The instant the dowager duchess and Gemma arrived, he threw open the door to greet them. Then, once they crossed the threshold, he didn't even give them a chance to settle into their bedchambers before he offered to give them a tour of the house.

It was unforgivable, he knew, but he couldn't seem to help it. He wanted Gemma to fall in love with Dunnock Park.

Much to his surprise and delight, Gemma immediately agreed to the tour.

This alteration from her usual hesitancy gave him hope to imagine that he was not the only one who had been thunderstruck. Normally, he was terrible at interpreting a woman's interest, as his past failures had clearly shown. But with Gemma, perhaps it would be different.

When they reached the gallery, the dowager duchess chose to linger at one end of the long paneled room while Sam and Gemma continued toward the other. Their synchronous steps echoed on the hardwood floor and up to the vaulted ceiling, bringing attention to the fact that she wasn't saying much. Still, he was beyond pleased to have her here. The urge to take her hand was so strong that he had to clasp his own behind his back like manacles.

Gemma was an irresistible ray of sunshine in her butter-cup yellow muslin, the sleeves and bodice embroidered with pale orange shells. The color of the thread reminded him of the string of coral she'd received from her aunt yesterday. He was now rather fond of that necklace.

"You're not wearing your aunt's gift," he said, his voice low. His gaze drifted to the dark wispy curls at her nape and his fingertips pulsed with the need to feel her skin again. "I would be more than glad to assist you."

She lifted her hand to the base of her throat. "No...I...it is too precious for me to wear every day."

He understood. Besides, he was distracted enough as it was, even without the visual reminder of their afternoon together. And perhaps she was distracted too. Often, when he looked over, he caught her plucking at a loose thread dangling from her gloves, her expression far too serious.

"I hope you found the road from Banfern Glenn to Dunnock Park fair," he said, trying to learn why she was unusually quiet. Could it be that she was nervous about being here?

"Quite," she offered, with another tug on that thread.

Since that wasn't much of a foundation for building a conversation, he tried again. "Last time I counted, there were forty-seven different varieties of trees along the way, leaves aplenty to examine under a microscope."

"Hmm."

He frowned, having expected a different response. Or really, any response at all. Was that thread so fascinating?

Though perhaps she was simply overly tired from their outing. After all, she had been traveling for days, which tended to leave a person exhausted. *That could be the reason*, he thought. All he knew was that he'd give anything to see her smile. And inspiration struck when they arrived at the next portrait.

"This fine fellow wearing a wig of such astounding glory is my four times great-grandfather," he said, puffing out his chest. "As you can see, he was rather fond of spotted capes."

Even though the bow shape of her mouth gave her a look of sly amusement, her eyes remained pensive. "Surely he donned this attire in the style of King Charles and solely for the portrait. Look, he even has the king's favorite spaniels by his side."

Sam shook his head, his expression a mask of severity. "Cats in costume. Great-grandfather hated dogs and merely had the artist take some liberties. Look, you can even see the curve of a cat's tail at the bottom of the portrait."

When she peered closer, rising on her toes and squinting, the chuckle he'd meant to withhold slipped out. She turned on him with a gasp and wagged her finger. "You cad! You were teasing me?"

He stepped back, holding his hands up in surrender. Here she was—the girl he'd been waiting to see. "I had to do something to make you smile."

"*Cats in costume*," she muttered under her breath, even as—*at last*—her lips curled upward. "You are completely ridiculous."

Sam could not argue. For her smile, he would play the fool. "Shall I continue and tell you about his wife, *Catriona*?"

But just as soon as he gestured to the next portrait, she looked down at her hands and tugged on that blasted thread again. "I have something I need to tell you, and I must do so before I lack the courage."

His elation was subdued instantly. "Yes, of course. Would you like to sit down first?"

She shook her head and faced him. Then, after drawing in a deep breath, she lifted her gaze to his. "I cannot stay."

He blinked. Surely he hadn't heard her correctly. "I do not understand."

"It is for the best that I leave Dunnock Park immediately."

No. He refused to believe it. There was so much more he wanted to show her—seven more generations of his family that he'd not introduced her to. He wanted to laugh about their elaborate costumes, knowing that Gemma would appreciate their historical significance. He wanted to talk to her about dozens of things that they'd barely had the opportunity to touch upon yesterday and the day before. And most important, he wanted her to meet his mother and father.

As it stood, his parents had expressed a fervent wish not to attend the party until the very end, claiming that they did not want to influence his decision. But he was beyond their influence at this point. "Have my manners been too forward and disagreeable? If so, I shall remedy it this very instant."

"You are perfect," she said earnestly, her gaze searching his. "The fault lies with me, in that I have not told you the entire truth behind the reason my aunt and I are traveling Surrey."

Now he truly was confused. Had he misread her smiles and laughter? "You said the holiday was for your enjoyment."

"That much was true. However, the full reason has more to do with my father. You see, when you did not recognize—"

"Pardon me, m'lord," the butler interrupted from the open archway, clearing his throat. "Two carriages have arrived. Do you still wish to greet your guests in the foyer? Or shall I have them wait in the parlor?"

Glancing over his shoulder to Mr. Fentum, standing as stiff as a barrel and dressed in dark livery, Sam was torn. The uncertainty in Gemma's eyes made him feel like he was running out of time, and he was desperate to grab hold of each moment with her. But it was like trying to capture the spear-shaped leaves of the willow in autumn before they reached the water.

She laid her hand on his arm. "Go. I should not keep you from your guests."

"I do not want you to leave," he said with indisputable firmness, tamping down every impulse to reach out and haul her against him.

The flesh around her eyes tightened, and two small, anxious furrows appeared between her brows. When she drew in a deep breath, he thought she would refuse him. But instead, she offered a patently reluctant nod.

"Then, perhaps my aunt and I could tour the gardens, and I will speak with you when it is more convenient."

He wanted to feel relief, believing that he had another opportunity to convince her to stay. Yet a powerful swell of unease tripped through him. It was impossible to forget how his prior experiences had not turned out as he'd hoped. And now, he would have an agonizingly long wait ahead of him before he learned whatever news Gemma was about to impart.

CHAPTER SIX

A steady succession of guests arrived, as if they'd collectively planned to descend on Dunnock Park at once. Sam received them, one after the other, but without his usual attentiveness. At the moment, he was thoroughly preoccupied with thoughts of Gemma.

What had she needed to tell him? From her worried expression, he knew it was not happy news. His worst fear was that she was promised to another. He seemed to have a knack for finding young women whose hearts were drawn to other men.

"My lord," Fentum said as he rushed back to the foyer, out of breath. After answering an urgent summons from the housekeeper, he looked somewhat haggard, his pomaded salt-and-pepper hair sticking out in places like a bird in molting season. "Lord Avery Hollander and Lord Bates Hollander insisted that their assigned bedchambers were inferior to each other's. Yet even after I explained that both bedchambers were identical, other than the fact that one was blue and the other burgundy, they were still displeased. After much talk of who had the superior view of the stables, I took the liberty of permitting them to exchange chambers."

"Very good. And in the future, allow me to field their grievances," Sam said, gritting his teeth. Leave it to the Hollander twins—or as he referred to them, *One* and *Two*—to wreak havoc among the servants just when Sam couldn't afford to step away and handle the matter himself. His friends often put up a fuss for the sole purpose of causing mischief. Feeling impatient, he then asked, "Did you happen to take note of whether or not the Dowager Duchess of Vale and her niece were still in the garden?"

Fentum smoothed an efficient gloved hand over his hair. "I believe I caught sight of a parasol as I passed the windows at the back of the house. Shall I send a maid to ask if they require refreshments?"

"I'll see to it," Sam said with a swift glance down the long arched hallway toward a set of mahogany French doors that eventually led to the garden. The distance seemed to span miles instead of strides. "In fact, give my welcome to the rest of the guests who will be arriving and let them know that I will see them this afternoon for tea on the terrace."

Without delaying any longer, he slipped away and headed straight for the gardens.

Once he reached the doorway, however, he stopped. Two other guests—in particular, Miss Ashbury and her mother, the Lady Tillmanshire—were sitting at a table on the terrace near a wall of white and yellow clematis. Not wanting to draw attention to his actions, Sam lingered out of sight while he scanned the extensive gardens.

"I wonder when Miss Leeds will come down from her chamber. I daresay her tardiness is giving me the run of Dunnock Park," Miss Ashbury said, likely not realizing she had an audience other than her mother.

A smirk pulled at Sam's mouth as he glanced over at the pair and saw Miss Ashbury touch her hand to the hat pinned at an angle over her coiffed auburn curls. While he liked women who bore a sense of inner confidence, he was never one for presumptive arrogance. Though from the audaciousness of her mother's elaborate bird's nest hat, he imagined the trait ran in the family.

"All the better for you, I should think," Lady Tillmanshire said in the round, superior tones of a student in elocution class. For a woman who'd only become a baroness last year after her merchant husband purchased his title, she'd adapted to society remarkably well. "Let the servants see how well you are suited for such a house and leave your *dearest friend* to fend for herself. Besides, she is likely plotting against you this very moment with that child of a stepmother, Lady Cantham. I do not like how they are always whispering to each other."

Miss Ashbury appeared unconcerned, her primary focus on using the tip of a fan to push an errant flower petal off the edge of the table, her face scrunched in disgust. "I have heard Miss Creighton and Miss Stapleton will also be in attendance."

"Mmm. Though it pains me to say it, I can see the appeal of Miss Stapleton. Not only is her father rich, but she is passably pretty with her country-cream complexion. Though her cheeks are too round, if you ask me. As for Miss Creighton"—the baroness tutted, the bird's nest teetering slightly—"well, one must account for an invitation out of pity."

Miss Ashbury nodded. "Indeed, she is quite as plain as a brown egg. And I don't believe her father has much of a fortune."

"Some young women, you will find, were simply born to become spinsters. I've heard she is a bluestocking as well," Lady Tillmanshire continued. "Fortunately, you need never be accused of such unseemly intelligence, and you will make a better match because of it."

"Perhaps even Lord Ellery."

"Just so," Lady Tillmanshire agreed, then continued in a hushed voice. "And as soon as we dispatch that foolish agreement your father made with that uncouth Lord Haggerty, all the better for us. I do not know what came over him to think of aligning our family with that man."

Sam frowned. He'd heard about the courtship agreement between Lord Haggerty and Miss Ashbury, but he'd been assured by Lord Tillmanshire himself that the matter had already been settled. If Sam had known that Miss Ashbury was still in an agreement with another man, he never would have invited her.

The only reason he considered Miss Ashbury for his guest list had been due to her professed interest in horticulture, but from the look of her discomfort from a mere petal, he wondered if that had been a falsehood as well.

The realization made him all the more thankful for Gemma. From all that he knew about her, she was not the least bit deceitful.

Attempting to tune out the rest of the petty conversation, Sam turned his gaze back to the garden, skimming past the roses, then followed the curvy border of the asters to the box-wood hedge.

When, after scanning the entire garden, he still could not find her, panic began to fill him. Surely Gemma wouldn't have gone without telling him first.

Then he spotted a familiar lace parasol at the back of the gardens, and he exhaled in relief. As long as she was still here, he had a chance to convince her to stay.

"The sooner the better," Miss Ashbury continued, "for my maid informed me moments after the bedchamber door closed that Lord Ellery invited *another* young woman and her aunt to join the party. Apparently, the servants are in a dither over their master's sudden fascination with this mystery debutante."

"You needn't worry," Lady Tillmanshire added, "for men are just as apt to fall out of fascination when someone far superior is within reach. Though, since my own maid was busy pressing our clothes for this evening, I had not heard this development. Did yours give the name of this unexpected rival?"

"She did not and only said that this woman arrived before any of us and was seen heading toward the gardens."

"Ah. That is the reason you required fresh air. My clever girl."

"I do believe that parasol must be attached to our quarry," Miss Ashbury said with a distinctly sharp edge to her voice.

Yet for Sam, their conversation droned on like the buzz of a pair of fat bumblebees nearby. His primary focus was on the white finial top of the parasol as it moved along the hedgerow. Anticipation thrummed in his pulse, and he took a moment to steel himself before he strode out into the garden.

Before he could, she appeared beneath the stone archway, looking slightly disheveled, beautiful, and perfectly at home. He grinned at the thought. Carrying her straw bonnet loosely in her hand, she let the sun caress her face and shoulders, her skin possessing a golden glow. She was not the type to preen for approval but was elegant in her own way, her limbs fluid and graceful. She paused to admire the flowers and plants, openly adoring them with an upward tilt to her lips and a brush of her fingertips over the leaves.

His own fingers tingled from the memory of her touch the day he'd picked the woodbines. He'd wanted to kiss her so much that he'd hardly been able to breathe. In fact, he wanted to do so right now—simply walk straight to her, pull her in his arms, and press his lips to hers.

Answering that inexorable urge, his body took an automatic step out onto the terrace. But when the breeze caught her pale yellow muslin, briefly molding the dress against her lithe form, caressing the curve of her hip and the feminine cradle between her slender thighs, he went stock still. Every beat of Sam's heart descended lower in thick succession as he struggled to fight a surge of intense arousal that was not proper for midday in the garden with guests nearby. And this time, he did not have a hat or a picnic basket to hide the evidence stirring beneath the fall front of his trousers.

"Do you know them, Mother?" Miss Ashbury asked, thankfully still unaware of his presence.

"Hmm. There is something familiar in the stature and gate of the elder woman with the parasol. If only I had my lorgnettes and then surely—*no*."

"What is it?" Miss Ashbury asked, more intrigued than startled.

"It cannot be, but it looks very like the Dowager Duchess of Vale."

"Oh, piffle, that is not all bad. Earning her approval would be a fine feather in my cap, after all."

"You misunderstand. That could only mean the young woman at her side is the scandalous Miss Desmond. Surely Lord Ellery would not think to invite someone of such bad blood to this gathering of superior *haute ton*." Lady Tillmanshire sniffed with clear disdain. "Why, if word got out, we could all be tainted by her mere presence."

While the distractions of Gemma's shape slipped into a different corner of Sam's mind, his attention fixed on the words *scandalous* and *bad blood*. Instantly, he knew that this had something to do with whatever Gemma had wanted to tell him.

Abruptly, a dire warning clambered through him. Had he allowed an impulse to cloud his judgment?

His uncertainty only increased when Gemma drew near and stepped out from beneath the rose arbor. At first, her gaze flared to life, brightening when she saw him. But that quickly changed when she glanced to the people at the table, and her expression fell, turning blank and colorless.

"Good day, Lady Tillmanshire," the dowager duchess said with a hauteur he hadn't heard before. The low tone sounded more like a warning than a greeting. "Miss Ashbury."

In a furor of feathers, the baroness rose from the table and straightened her shoulders. With a snap of her hand against her side, she bid her daughter to do the same. "And to you, Your Grace."

Then, without a word of greeting to Gemma, Lady Tillmanshire and Miss Ashbury turned on their heels to leave. Yet they stopped short when they saw Sam standing near the doorway.

"Lord Ellery," Lady Tillmanshire said, her expression altering from disdain to something just short of fawning, leaving her features in a confused, crooked state. "Please forgive our rapid departure from the terrace. My daughter has a sudden headache. Though I wonder if you might escort us back to our chambers?"

No doubt the busybody wanted to fill him in on all the details. However, Sam would rather hear it from Gemma's own lips.

Looking over his shoulder, he saw a footman carrying an empty silver tray toward the kitchens. "Barnes, if you would be so good as to escort Lady Tillmanshire and Miss Ashbury to their rooms…"

The footman nodded. Then, saying nothing more to the baroness and her daughter, Sam strode forward, determined to find out what Gemma was hiding.

"…*the scandalous Miss Desmond.*"

Icy dread dowsed Gemma as she looked from Sam to the older woman with the broad tan hat, heavily browed scowl, and an overbite that resembled a camel's. Panic quickened her pulse, the sound of it like a windstorm in her ears, drowning out whatever else the woman said. All Gemma knew was that it made Sam frown. His brow furrowed in confusion as his gaze met hers.

In that instant, she knew she'd betrayed his trust.

She'd waited too long to confess. Now, everything she said would cast a shadow over their entire acquaintance, and he would believe her to be the most secretive and conniving of all women.

Her stomach churned at the thought of his despising her. He had every right to turn his back on her and follow the women who'd shown their disapproval.

Yet he surprised her by walking forward. "Your Grace, if I may have a moment of Miss Desmond's time," he said without taking his eyes from Gemma, and searching her countenance all the while.

"Of course, Lord Ellery, though I shall keep to the garden as well." From her clipped tone, it was clear that Aunt Edith's hackles were standing on end. Right then, she was very like a white feathered cockatoo, protecting her hatchling.

Sam inclined his head and lifted his hand, gesturing to the garden path.

When he did not say anything, Gemma knew he was waiting for her to begin. But *where* to begin? Back to when her mother died? Or when her father decided to remove Gemma from the only family she'd known to begin a life of deceit in the desert? Perhaps she should start with the years of her father's gambling, and how that led him to a group of men who had a talent for making forgeries and passing them off as artifacts. Living a life in the company of scoundrels, there were so many instances she could name.

However, in order to clear her own conscience, it was most important to start where she'd deceived Sam.

"I never intended to tell you my name at all," she confessed quietly, just audible above the rasp of her skirts brushing against the stalks of lavender beside the path. "Our meeting at the pond was so strange and perfect that I did not want to ruin it by revealing my surname. As you've likely realized, it causes revulsion in anyone who speaks it."

He looked up at the sky and, after a lengthy exhale, shook his head. "If you never intended to tell me, then you must not have imagined ever seeing me again."

"I was not arrogant enough to believe that I left you with the same pleasurable impression you imprinted on me," she said, even though that was not entirely the truth. She had dreamed of meeting him once more, but at the time, it felt like a fool's fantasy.

"Yet surely when I arrived at the inn shortly after you and your aunt had, you knew the truth."

Hearing his frustration in the harsh edge of his tone, she nearly reached out to set her hand upon his arm but drew back. It was too late for such familiarity. A vast emptiness seemed to open inside of her, a void telling her that she had lost what she might have had.

"And I was overcome with joy to learn that I was wrong. But even then, I thought that too was doomed to be short-lived, once you learned my surname." She swallowed down a rush of guilt. "When my aunt introduced us, and you did not immediately recognize the name, I considered myself fortunate that, at last, I was able to escape it. I even told myself it was a harmless omission."

"The name of Desmond did spark some familiarity, but not enough to warrant the reaction I just witnessed from Lady Tillmanshire," he growled, expelling a hiss between his teeth. Then he suddenly stopped on the path and turned to her, his severe expression pinning her in place. "Your explanation is plotting a slow course and leaves me to conjure dozens of reasons in the space of each step we take. Please tell me now if your name is attached to a husband or to a man to whom you are promised."

Taken aback by his assumption, she blinked for clarity. Was *that* the worst nightmare he could imagine? He did not leap to conclusions that she was ill bred but only wondered if another man might have laid claim to her heart before he could?

That thumping organ beneath her breast swelled, giving rise to a renewed urge to fling herself at him, arms wide. She kept her face a practiced mask of severity while inside she was gaily clapping like a lunatic. Then, to keep herself still, she clasped her hands together. "It is not."

He seemed to consider this as he drew in a breath and nodded. "Are your affections otherwise engaged?"

"They are not," she said on a breath, chiding herself for wanting to smile and hold on to this moment. However, knowing what terrible news she must impart kept her sober. "Nor am I free to allow such an occurrence."

She had to keep walking. Facing him, standing as they were and able to see every nuance of his open expression, made her want to delay the inevitable. So she turned and continued on the path as he kept pace beside her.

"Do you recall the London news event in which someone kidnapped and attempted to murder Miss Adeline Pimm?" She shuddered at her own question, recalling every detail of how her father had ordered one of his men to put Miss Pimm—now, the Countess of Wolford—inside a crate with a marble bust and to toss her to the bottom of the Thames.

"I do. Your cousin Lord Wolford borrowed my horse that very morning," Sam said, his brow furrowed as if in memory. Clearly, he was starting to put the pieces together on his own.

Emotion seized her throat as Sam's brow flattened, and he stared down at her with some unnamed expression. She had not seen this one before, and it made her nervous not to know what cards he held.

"Your assistance that day likely saved my cousin-in-law's life. Adeline is a dear friend now, and I have you to thank," she added quickly, knowing that they were reaching the end of their brief acquaintance. She felt pinpricks at the corners of her eyes as tears threatened. It was unpardonable to feel sorry for herself and even worse to reveal it.

She did what she could to keep the tears at bay. Straightening her shoulders, she said, "My father is Albert Desmond, the man who orchestrated the events of that day. The very name I hold is a black mark against my entire family. And I cannot, in good conscience, tarnish your household with my presence."

Before she lost her battle and gave in to tears, she turned to escape past the hedgerow.

But Sam did not let her get far. Taking hold of her arm, firmly but gently, he stopped her. "Where are you going?"

Still turned away from him, she shook her head. Surely, she did not need to explain any more. Her fate was evident to everyone who knew the story. "First to fetch my aunt, then back to Banfern Glenn, and after that, I could not say."

He didn't release her. Instead, he stepped closer and settled both hands over the sleeves at her shoulders. The warm, comforting pressure breached the door where she'd locked her tears, and down they tumbled in heavy drops that dotted the bodice of her dress with small, wet ocher ovals.

"Please, Sam, just let me go."

"I cannot," he said softly. "By your own admission, you are unable to escape the stain upon your surname. So then why bother running at all? You could just as easily stay here."

"*Stay?*" If she weren't so miserable, she would laugh. Lifting her hand, she surreptitiously wiped away the self-serving tears. "Your own name is now in jeopardy because of my foolish"—she stopped herself before the word *wish* escaped her lips—"and fraudulent scheme against you."

"A *scheme* against me?" He let out a low laugh that tempted her to lean back against him in order to feel it rumble inside her. "What? Had you plotted to marry me in order to alter your name?"

She could not answer him. There had been a moment when she'd thought about it. Truth be told, she'd imagined it more than once, believing that if anyone had the nature to forgive her for such a plot, he would have. Eventually.

"By your silence I am left to wonder if that same thought"—he hesitated, as if unsure—"occurred to you."

"Only briefly," she said in haste. "I never would have gone through with it."

"And why not?" He almost sounded affronted.

Because I'm already too fond of you, she admitted to herself, squeezing her eyes shut.

"Would you mind repeating that? The breeze must have carried away your whisper."

Her eyes sprang open. Had she muttered that aloud? After all the years of carefully shielding her emotions and thoughts from others, this was the absolute worst time to lose control of them.

Embarrassed, she cleared her throat to recover, thankful that he hadn't heard her. "Because you deserve someone better than I am."

"I preferred your first answer. Then again, that quiet admission might have been part of this...*scheme* of yours." Strangely, he sounded more contemplative than angry by the supposition. "Which could mean that you began your plot at the pond, making sure to lure me with your wit and a fine display of leg."

She blushed, the remaining tears drying in splotches on her heated cheeks. Again, she tried to pull free, but his deceptively gentle hold would not allow it. "You should not mention that you saw me en déshabillé."

"Of course, you are right," he said, all seriousness, his thumbs moving over the crests of her shoulders in slow, hypnotizing sweeps. "I will not *speak* of it but only *think* of it fondly."

"If you are trying to make me laugh, it won't work."

"Oh, I think it might. After all, I was able to get you to smile, wasn't I?" He turned her then, the evidence displayed on her lips as she gazed up at him in wonder. There was something about him that soothed her tattered nerves and hushed her dire thoughts.

But did she have a right to feel even an ounce of happiness with him?

Abruptly she sobered. "I apologize for deceiving you."

He shook his head, his gaze tender as he reached up and settled his hand beneath her chin. Then, withdrawing a handkerchief from the inside pocket of his coat, he carefully blotted away the last traces of dampness from her cheeks. "Gemma, I can think of no person who introduces herself by cataloguing the sins and misdeeds of her family. If that became the practice, then I daresay, people would be so frightened from making new acquaintances they would hardly leave their houses."

"That is no excuse. Because of my presence at Dunnock Park, your own very good name may fall under scrutiny."

He tilted up her face, searching her gaze. "Is that what you have endured—gossip and castigations—since you arrived in London?" Then his expression turned hard, his jaw set. "Well, no more—not while you are here."

Wait a moment. She could not have heard him correctly. "You still want me to stay?"

"Of course you are staying," he said, as if there had never been a question in the first place.

She was stunned by his easy acceptance and readiness to defend her. Not to mention enthralled by his utter confidence. The weight that had been pressing upon her for months lifted somewhat, making her feel lighter. Hopeful.

"You know nothing of me. So how can you believe me faultless, especially after all that I have told you?"

"Many people have experienced dark deeds in one form or another, but that does not put the fault on their shoulders," he said, shifting closer, his thumb brushing over her chin in a tender caress. "Do we blame the puffed dandelion for losing its seeds in a storm?"

She could scarcely breathe. Each time he touched her, she felt so completely connected to him, as if they were of the same mind and body, with the same frissons of sensation that begged for a closer proximity. That anxious churning in her stomach suddenly transformed into tightly wound spirals, and she swayed slightly toward him.

Then, anchoring herself, she placed her hand over his and cupped it briefly to her cheek. It didn't even occur to her that this was too intimate a gesture for a garden in the full light of day, let alone between an unchaperoned debutante and a marriage-minded viscount. All she knew was that it felt exactly right to be here with him.

His gaze dipped to her mouth as the tip of his thumb slipped into the sensitive valley between her chin and the flesh of her bottom lip, making her lips feel plump and tender and desperate for the pressure of his. If she would have known how perfect it felt to be close to him, she may very well have schemed her way into his party and onto his list of potential brides.

"More than ever," he said, his voice low, "I believe it is my duty to help you fulfill the plan you made with your aunt."

"To...to *marry* you?" She gasped, wondering if she'd spoken aloud again. Her blush sparked instantly to flame, and she dropped her hand, taking a step back. "But that was merely a...a passing thought, and I never fully intended to...to—"

Her stammers stopped abruptly when he flashed a smile, the warm gleam in his eyes doing strange, wonderful things to her.

"*Or* I might have been speaking of your intention to enjoy this holiday trip to the fullest."

"Oh yes, of course," she said on a breath, more mortified than she cared to admit. She shifted from one foot to the other, knowing her cheeks must have turned eight different shades of red. "But there is one thing you have not considered. By playing host to Albert Desmond's daughter, you might very well ruin your chance to find a bride among your guests."

His gaze flitted sideways to the whitewashed cottage just down the hill and to the gardener who stood outside, trimming a conical juniper. "It is a risk I'm willing to take."

Gemma only hoped he would not regret his decision.

CHAPTER SEVEN

The following afternoon, the guests gathered on the lawn for a rousing game of ground billiards. Sam stood off to one side of the manicured lane, having missed the hazard and ending in the rough. He wasn't one to complain, however. Not with Gemma nearby and standing with her back to him, the heart-shaped curve of her derriere on display through lavender muslin as she bent at the waist in order to line up her mallet for the shot.

Until this moment, he never knew how much he enjoyed the game.

"So who's the girl, Ellery?"

Sam frowned at the interruption. He'd been careful to linger in the shadows beneath the canopy of elms that bordered either side of the alley, believing the direction of his gaze was well concealed. Leave it to the dark-haired man who now joined him to find him out.

Lord Asher Holt had arrived before dawn that morning and straight from a house of ill repute, by the look and smell of him. Now, however, he was cleanly shaven, pressed into a dove gray coat, and wearing his signature black cravat that matched the gleaming onyx color of his irises. "Still in your pre-mourning garb, I see."

Holt's mouth twisted in a wry smirk. "My father is bound to die at some point. I'm merely showing my respects ahead of time. After he's in the ground, I plan to bury all my black cravats with him; wear only gleaming, angelic white; and then live a life of sainthood."

With a chuckle, Sam lifted his mallet and stepped to the side. "Warn me the next time you're about to spew an abominable falsehood. I should not wish to be too near the spot of your smiting."

Holt glanced heavenward, his jaw set in stone and his eyes hard, as if in a dare. "One born to a *Luciferian* father quickly loses all hope of divine intervention." Then his mask of boredom returned as he lowered his gaze to the players scattered about the lawn. "You didn't answer the question—*who's the girl?*"

Sam was hoping he hadn't noticed. "There are many young women here. At the middle hazard stands Miss Creighton, doing her best to hide beneath that enormous straw bonnet as Hollander *Two* stands nearby, doubtless teasing her to make her miss her shot." Hollander *One* was busy entertaining the chaperones, having been caught early on by Lady Tillmanshire, who wanted to know about his fortune. "On the far right, behind Miss Creighton, is the dimple-cheeked Miss Stapleton with her father. The latter of the two appears to be taking this game rather seriously, considering how he tossed a handful of grass in the air to gauge the direction of the wind."

While Holt chuckled at the sight, Sam glanced to Gemma just as she sent her ball reeling with a sharp crack of her mallet, whizzing through the arch. His fist clenched with a sense of shared triumph before he reluctantly had to return his attention to the others.

"The trio still deciding who should go first among them is Miss Ashbury, Miss Leeds, and Lady Cantham, her new stepmother," he said dismissively.

Holt arched one eyebrow in hope. "Dowries enough to tempt me?"

"By your standards, the daughter of Midas would leave you wanting."

"Don't be too certain. After all, a young woman turned into gold would be unable to plague me with demands; therefore, I may find myself quite content," Holt said with a smirk. "Though I'm not opposed to settling for a...cousin of that family. Is there a Miss Midas among them?"

Sam glanced at the group. "I've heard that Miss Stapleton has a solid ten thousand pounds."

Holt made a sound of disgust. "I'd need ten times that to pay off Father's debts." Even so, he took a second look at Miss Stapleton. "Why the hell did you invite me?"

"Solely to ensure that the bride I choose witnesses what horrors await her on the marriage mart, should she not accept my suit," Sam said, deadpan.

In truth, he wanted Holt to enjoy himself, perhaps to find happiness, *and* to stop planning his life around his father's death. That was no way to live.

Holt smirked. "But what about the debutante you didn't mention—the one who receives wary, if not lethal, glances from the others? Am I to assume that she is separated not only from the main party but from your list of candidates as well?"

So Holt had noticed too. Sam had wondered if he was simply being overly protective of Gemma, especially after last night and the silent treatment she'd received at dinner. He did not like the way the others were still keeping their distance from her, as if the acts of her father were a disease she wore upon her skin. It made no sense to him. If they would only give her a chance, they would see how clever and good-natured she was.

Although he retained hope that the shy Miss Creighton and the sunny Miss Stapleton would come around. At least they'd tried to speak to Gemma. Lady Tillmanshire, Miss Ashbury, Lady Cantham, *and* Miss Leeds, however, had doggedly interrupted every attempt by diverting conversation to another topic. They'd even trod on his own efforts. And with Gemma's place at the far end of the long table, he'd been unable to come to her aid without, he feared, bringing more spiteful behavior down upon her.

If he had the chance to revisit the past, his house party would only include the dowager duchess and Gemma.

"Assume nothing of the sort," Sam said to Holt. "She is, most definitely, on the list."

"Dowry?" Holt shot an appraising look across the lane.

Sam stepped forward, turning to block his friend's view, and set the head of his mallet on the ground firmly between his feet. "If there is a dowry, it would be quite small. Nothing to interest you."

Those onyx eyes twinkled with mischief. "Now, I find myself all the more interested. Say, does this poor creature have a name?"

Before Sam could answer, he heard Gemma's voice from behind him.

"Lord Ellery, I believe it's your turn."

Sam pivoted on his heel to see the object of their exchange not three steps from him, and his irritation at Holt evaporated from the warmth of her smile. She raised her hand to shield her eyes from the sun, her skin glowing beneath the golden rays. The sight filled him with a powerful urge to pull her into the shade, press his lips to her bare flesh, and feel the heat rising from her skin. Here in the full light, he could see the spots of pink on each swell where the sun had left its mark on her, and he felt a ridiculous rise of jealousy for the blazing star, wanting to leave his own mark instead. When he gave in and briefly allowed himself to imagine just that, his mouth suddenly went dry.

At the base of her throat, the faintest shimmer of perspiration drew his attention to the enticing V-shaped notch. If he were to dip his tongue into that spot, would she taste of warm spice and salt from her exertions? Or would she be more like the woodbine and have the essence of sunshine and sweet morning dew on her skin?

He had an inescapable desire to know.

She touched her fingertips there, and he swallowed. "Am I getting pink? Aunt Edith is forever scolding me for being out of doors without my bonnet. I should hate to give her a reason to be right—" Her eyes widened slightly, and her cheeks tinged to a dark rose. "Oh, you are not alone. I did not see that you were standing with…otherwise I would not have spoken so…regardless, I should not have asked you to comment on my…you know, you could be a gentleman and stop me at any time."

Sam grinned at the way she wagged her finger at him when she was flustered. "But you are doing marvelously on your own."

"The invisible Lord Holt at your service," Holt interrupted, stepping forward with a bow. "It seems as if the two of you are old friends, and yet Ellery was in the middle of telling me absolutely nothing about you. Not even your name. I cannot account for it, only to say that it stands to wonder if he's trying to keep you all to himself."

"I'm certain that is not the case," Gemma said in a rush. "Lord Ellery and I have only just met, you see, so there is very little for him to know and an even smaller amount for him to tell."

Holt shook his head. "Impossible. My friend is far too cautious to invite a stranger to his party. He prefers watchfulness to spontaneity and likely has a list of interests and commonalities about each of his guests tucked away in his desk."

Gemma tilted her head to study Sam. "Is this true about the list?"

He had every name on it but one.

Sam shrugged. "If you'll recall, I mentioned having a cautious nature soon after we met."

"Yes, but I thought"—she hesitated, looking askance at Holt before she continued in a lower voice—"you were trying to charm me so that I would accept your invitation."

Holt clutched Sam's shoulder. "All the years of uncontrollable—oftentimes brutal—honesty, and at long last, it has finally worked in your favor. Now, be a good man and introduce me at once."

Sam hesitated, wanting to keep her all to himself. Holt's dark and aloof nature had always appealed to women in a way that Sam had never fully understood. Seemingly sensible debutantes and matrons alike fawned over and flirted with him, dropping fans, handkerchiefs, and whatnot at his feet in order to gain his attention.

While Sam never lacked for admiration and had even been hailed as the *toast of the ton* this past Season, he'd often worried that it had been because of Holt's absence. Was it too much to ask for a young woman to lose her wits, just a little, over him?

"This is Miss Desmond," he said, biting down on the urge to claim her as his. *My Miss Desmond. My Gemma.*

"Desmond..." Holt's brow furrowed. "Why does that name sound familiar?"

Beside him, Gemma stiffened, her delicate features set as if cast in hardened clay. There was a sudden pallor to her skin as well, and the light dimmed from her eyes. In that instant, her demeanor altered completely from the relaxed state he knew into that of a fortress prepared for attack. "My surname is that of a criminal's. Likely, you recall it from the papers."

Feeling his own man-at-arms arise within him, Sam locked his jaw and straightened his shoulders. He was prepared to rail at Holt if he made a single derogatory comment.

Holt shook his head and arched that brow once more. "Interesting conversation starter, but no, that isn't where I've heard it. I pay no attention to the papers—ghastly, depressing news, day after day."

"Then I believe you know her cousins, the Duke of Vale and the Earl of Wolford," Sam suggested, his voice edged with warning. "Her aunt, the Dowager Duchess of Vale, is just across the lawn."

"Ah! I know Wolford well, indeed. Even though I have been away from town for months, I heard the rascal was strangled by the marriage noose recently."

A breath left Gemma in a soft whoosh, and the rigid column of her spine relaxed into a softer curve. "My cousin wears his noose with great contentment. In recalling the years Liam vowed to live a full life and not marry until he reached his sixtieth year, I am thankful that he found his bride much sooner."

"Some men can afford contentment," Holt said in a tone of wounded mystery that typically elicited female interest, or in the very least a desire to soothe him.

Sam held his breath as Gemma's lips parted for her response. Then to his surprise, she turned her full attention to him.

"Ellery, are you going to force me to play your turn and then my own? I will, you know," she said with a cheeky smirk. "And you'd likely end up the better for it. After all, none of my strikes has ended in the rough."

"It wasn't my fault. There was a low iron arch in the way of a perfectly good shot."

She laughed. "The trick is to go through the hazards as if they were never there at all."

"I'll try to remember that," he said, smiling. In that moment he could have sworn the sun shone a little brighter on the alley, and it filled him with the hope that he wasn't imagining her interest in him.

L ater that afternoon, the women gathered on the stone terrace while the gentlemen visited the stables. Green-painted wrought-iron chairs sat in groupings of four, surrounding several small tables of the like.

From their spot, Aunt Edith and Gemma had a perfect view of the stables through a border of vibrantly blooming smoke trees. Miss Creighton and her aunt, *also* Miss Creighton, along with Miss Stapleton occupied the nearest table. Then sitting farthest from the group were Lady Tillmanshire, Miss Ashbury, Miss Leeds, and her young stepmother, Lady Cantham.

It did not take long for Gemma to realize that these four were determined to ensure the near-biblical destruction of enjoyment. In fact, if there were such a book as a *Bible for House Parties*—and a book of Revelation therein—then these women would be the *four horsewomen of the house-party apocalypse*.

Last evening, Gemma had noted that the Misses Creighton were a timid pair, both pale and brunette but with watchful eyes, the younger possessing lashes as thick as mink fur. All the better to shield her shy glances toward the Hollander twins, Gemma imagined. Both *One* and *Two*, as Sam referred to his friends, had flanked the bookish Miss Honoria Creighton at the table and, through their antics, had done their best to coax her out of her shell. Yet every time Miss Leeds or Miss Ashbury had spoken, she would startle and hastily look down to her plate.

On the bright side, Honoria Creighton and the sunny Miss Aurora Stapleton appeared to be bosom companions. The latter of the two had nearly spoken to Gemma at dinner. They'd sat across from each other, their gazes and smiles colliding each time the Hollander twins shared an amusing anecdote. And while the gentlemen were good to include everyone in conversation, each time Gemma, Miss Creighton, or Miss Stapleton had the opportunity to speak, one of the *four horsewomen* had cut off their words most rudely.

For Sam's sake, Gemma had kept her comments to herself.

Today, however, biting her tongue was proving to be far more difficult.

"Your Grace," Lady Tillmanshire began, her voice loud enough to send a flock of nutshell-brown willow warblers scattering to the sky, "I hope your nephew Lord Wolford and his new bride are faring well after their unspeakable ordeal."

Not one to be fooled by false concern, Aunt Edith offered no thanks but merely said, "Quite well," and sipped her tea.

Lady Tillmanshire, however, remained seated on her warhorse, not dissuaded from her topic. She pursed her thick lips over her camel-overbite. "I cannot imagine how difficult it must have been to know that *your own* brother-in-law was nearly responsible for the countess's death."

Miss Ashbury tilted her head and primped her auburn curls, sending a smug grin in their direction. But all Gemma could think about was how fortunate Miss Ashbury was to not favor her mother in looks. Though it was a little disconcerting to know that someone so vicious could be so pretty. Worse, she was quite good at concealing her true nature whenever the gentlemen were around. Gemma only hoped that Sam would see through it.

As for the others at the table, Lady Cantham was a reputed beauty from last Season. Though Miss Leeds didn't seem to mind that her stepmother was only two years her senior. They were thick as thieves. Both of the women were slender, possessing pale blonde hair and fair complexions, but Miss Leeds's features were somewhat flatter—her mouth broad, her nose shallow—and on the odd occasion, she lisped like a viper disturbed from its basket.

Growing up primarily in the desert, Gemma had always been wary of snakes.

In response to Lady Tillmanshire's comment, Aunt Edith turned slowly and offered a glacial stare. "There now. Are you satisfied that everyone present knows of his evil deeds? Good. We wouldn't want anyone to misunderstand the point you were trying to make."

With a blanket of conjecture laid out plainly, the Misses Creighton and Miss Stapleton slid wary—but somewhat sympathetic—glances in Gemma's direction. Then, with the excuse of too much sun, the elder Miss Creighton suggested that she, her niece, and Miss Stapleton might rest for a time before dinner.

Gemma was sorry to see them go. She might have retired as well, if not for the fact that leaving would give the impression that the *four* had succeeded in running her off as well. Therefore, she decided that she would remain in this very spot. Until the end of days, if need be.

The hard truth of battle.

That evening, Gemma chose not to join the others in the parlor after dinner. She'd had her fill of close-quarters condescension for the past day and a half.

So instead, she tiptoed toward the stairs and hoped that no one would spot her.

"Surely that is not Miss Desmond sneaking upstairs."

Gemma stopped on the first step, her thoughts pleasantly interrupted by Sam's sudden appearance. Stepping out of the partially opened doorway of the parlor, he crossed his arms but gave her a teasing smirk.

"*Sneaking* is such a close cousin to *lurking*. I prefer…*quietly treading*," she whispered, wanting to maintain a semblance of privacy here in the hallway.

He did not stop moving toward her until there was only a curved banister between them. It was impossible not to notice how their faces were now at the same level. Should either of them be struck with a sudden passionate urge to press their mouths together…well, their proximity made it quite convenient.

If it were any other man, she would have taken an automatic step back, not wanting to allow for any untoward ideas. Yet with Sam, she had plenty of her own. And his heated glance down to her lips told her that his thoughts were similarly engaged.

"We are just about to begin our evening's entertainment," he said, the timbre of his voice low and intimate, his dark pupils reflecting the sconce light.

Without conscious thought, she caught herself listing forward. Even in still night air, he smelled of fresh summer wind and the warm, spiced essence of the earth baked in sunlight. She couldn't resist breathing in deeper.

"I know, but I took the liberty of pilfering your library for an interesting book, and I plan to spend time reading in my bedchamber. Well, not *my* bedchamber but the bedchamber you chose for me," she quickly corrected. Though her amendment didn't sound any better. And why couldn't she stop saying *bedchamber*?

Her pulse accelerated under his intense scrutiny, beating raggedly at her throat and harder beneath her breasts.

Then, realizing that she might have sounded as if she wasn't pleased with his choice, she continued. "The soft shade of blue makes for a lovely bedchamber"—there she went *again*—"and I especially like the cozy window seat. I cannot imagine a more perfect spot for reading."

He drew in a breath, his nostrils flaring as his gaze climbed the stairs as if, for an instant, he imagined joining her. So, of course, she thought of it too. The pair of them ensconced in the snug window seat, side by side, his arm brushing hers by accident as he turned the page of a book. Gentleman that he was, he would offer an apology. In turn, she would lift her face to absolve him of any fault, which would leave her at the perfect angle to receive his kiss. But would she let him?

The answer was embarrassingly easy. Yes, most assuredly *yes*.

"Do you like my library as well?" he asked, cleverly maneuvering the topic away from bedchambers.

It was for the best, she supposed. Her imagination was getting out of hand. "Very much, indeed. It is full of more books on history than I've ever seen in one place. We did not have many books when I was younger, so I am determined to read as many as I can. Though I will be lucky to get through one shelf before the party ends."

It was a shame she could not stay long enough to read them all.

He lifted his hand to rest it on the polished rail between them, the blunt tips of his fingers curling around to her side, bringing him a little bit closer. Of their own volition, her slippers shuffled nearer, her toes tipping over the rolled edge of the runner.

"I am glad you like it." The way he searched her gaze, she sensed he wasn't simply speaking about the room that inhabited his shelves, but his selection, his tastes, and perhaps even him. "But why not read in the parlor instead of in your bedchamber?"

Oh dear. Now she was thinking about bedchambers again, her mind racing past snug window seats and directly to the kissing. Her lips were tingling so fiercely that she had to press them together, and wait a minute—had she imagined it, or had he emphasized the words *your bedchamber*?

Her heart thumped so hard she was certain he could hear it. She hugged the book to her breast to muffle the sound and glanced over his shoulder to the open door. Her thoughts were wholly improper. "I had better not."

His expression hardened. "If anyone has been unkind or made you feel unwelcome in my home, then I will—"

On impulse, she laid her hand over his, and though she startled and tingled at the intimacy, she did not pull away. "It is nothing like that. Under the circumstances, your guests have been pleasant"—the *four horsewomen* were careful to keep their insults out of his earshot—"which is a debt I owe to you. You are well respected among your peers. I can never thank you enough for the joy you've brought to my aunt and to me."

He curved his thumb over her hand and tugged gently. "Then have more of it and come with me into the parlor. Bring your book, if you like."

Your book—why did those words sound so full of promise? Likely, the frissons of awareness teeming through her whenever he was near were starting to addle her brain. When he looked at her with such protective tenderness—something that had been absent for most of her life—she felt that everything and anything was possible. That she would have someone by her side, helping her to stand tall during the moments when she wasn't particularly strong. And that her life could start again, right here, right now.

It was a dangerous fantasy.

She shook her head. "I am afraid that, should I sit in the parlor, someone may ask me to play cards."

"Ah." His face transformed with his broad, easy grin. "Then if your reluctance comes from a lack of knowing the game, I should be more than glad to be your tutor."

For a moment, she contemplated an innocent pretense of knowing nothing about card play, for a wholly selfish purpose. However, that would not be honest or fair. *Drat.* "I would only be too happy if that were the reason."

His brow furrowed in confusion. "Then what is?"

Instead of excusing herself and ending their discourse, she decided to share the truth with him, even while knowing what it might cost her.

Reluctantly, she slid her hand free, her fingertips inadvertently brushing the crisp golden hairs near his wrist before she pulled away. Absent of his touch and warmth, she curled her hand into a fist.

"The problem is that I excel at card play, and the reason for it is quite scandalous." She drew in a fortifying breath before she continued. "Regardless, I cannot alter the facts. My father spent many years in gaming hells, and some owned by *associates* who did not mind having his daughter sit beside him. Many thought it was a lark to teach me how to play, keeping me occupied when my father was next to me, losing whatever fortune we might have had. During that time, I learned tricks from cheats and sleight-of-hand artists and even helped to spot the crooks who kept cards up their sleeves.

"And while I want to assure you that I do not condone cheating or practice it myself, the things that I have learned make it appear as though I do." She swallowed, preparing herself to see the look of horror that would surely cross Sam's expression any second now. "I cannot help but study people. By their expressions and gestures, and without giving it much thought, I can usually guess which cards they hold."

But, once again, Sam surprised her.

"That's marvelous, if you ask me," he said immediately and without even the smallest hint of abhorrence. "I find myself rather envious of the skill of reading people. I've no luck at it myself."

In her opinion, he was always on target with her thoughts… but she couldn't think about that now.

Reeling from his response, her breath staggered out of her lungs. "There are many who would believe that my upbringing, as well as the *out-of-the-ordinary* lessons I learned, were unseemly for a young woman, if not barbaric."

"I do not believe that," he said, reaching through the railing to take her hand again, his fingers dipping to the center of her fist, opening her grasp, and setting off a torrent of heated flutters. "You fascinate me, Gemma. And I don't want you ever to hide who you are. Not with me."

A beat of silent expectation stretched between them. Feeling safe, free from censure, and a thousand other pleasant emotions, she wrapped her fingers around his hand and nodded, unsure that her voice wouldn't break with her answer.

"I want to know everything"—he grinned and tugged her closer—"especially how to best Holt at the tables."

CHAPTER EIGHT

The following evening, Gemma went directly to the library again after dinner. As a happy coincidence, Sam soon followed, and they shared a few precious minutes alone. Well…not completely alone. The door was open, and Aunt Edith lingered in the hall, but Gemma's heart didn't know the difference. That lopsided whirring sensation began the instant he walked into the room.

Because of the *four horsewomen* and their constant interference, this was the first opportunity Gemma had to speak with Sam or even breathe the same air. Yet seeing him move toward her, his gait sure and direct, none of that mattered anymore.

"Have you found a book you fancy, Miss Desmond?" he asked with an almost rakish lift of his brow.

"Indeed," she said, not looking away from him. Then she quickly realized that she wasn't holding a book.

By the flash of his grin, Sam noticed too. "I'm glad."

She felt flustered and hot beneath his gaze, beneath her skin. Touching her hand to her throat, she found it ever-so-slightly damp with perspiration. "It's rather warm this evening."

"After living in the desert, I should think you would be accustomed to the heat." As he spoke, his hungry gaze dipped to follow the path of her fingers.

She found herself tilting her head, her fingertips lingering, imagining they were his. "The evenings were much cooler."

"Do you prefer that climate, or do you like it here?"

As with most of their exchanges, she sensed there was another layer underneath his question, a way for him to gain an understanding of her thoughts. "I prefer the weather in Surrey the best of all, and at Dunnock Park especially. It is perfect in every way."

Pleasure filled his expression, as if he'd known she meant that she liked *him* best of all, that *he* was perfect in every way. He took a step closer until they were standing toe to toe, his gaze darkening, drifting to her lips, and she knew he intended to kiss her.

She wasn't about to stop him.

Then suddenly there was a commotion in the hall, followed by Lord Holt's voice asking, "Wouldn't you prefer the parlor over the library, my lady?"

Sam took a step back, and Gemma turned to face the shelves, right before Lady Tillmanshire and Miss Ashbury spilled through the doorway.

The baroness began simpering and fawning immediately. "Lord Ellery, how clever you are to know the premier time of the day to take a tour among the shelves."

When the baroness and her daughter linked arms and began to saunter around the room—without even bothering to pick up a single book—Gemma assumed that her time with Sam was at an end.

Ever the consummate host, Sam politely responded to Lady Tillmanshire but then turned back to Gemma. "Miss Desmond, since you are so fond of history, I thought you might also enjoy this."

He handed her a book from the shelf in front of him, his fingers brushing against the bare skin exposed above the lace edge of her mitts. When she looked down and saw the book was on botany rather than history, she realized he'd done this solely to touch her.

For this reason, Gemma vowed to wear fingerless mitts every single day. Thankfully, Berta had brought back a fresh pair from the village when she picked up the—previously horrifying but now fondly—stained muslin from the laundress. The dress was now a lovely shade of dark rose that would be perfect for a special occasion.

"This room requires a feminine touch, my dear," Lady Tillmanshire announced to her daughter, her voice ringing like the blade of an ax hitting stone. "A proper wife might improve upon the furnishings, draperies, and add trinkets to the shelves to make them more enticing. You have always had a good eye for such things."

Gemma exchanged an amused glance with Sam and pursed her lips in thoughtful acknowledgment. Obviously, the baroness was trying to plant the seed of enticement.

Wanting a way to continue their encounter, a thought came to her. She still had yet to mention her observations of Lord Holt at the card table. So she too plucked a random book from the shelf and handed it to him, their fingers surreptitiously tangling. "And this book was quite interesting, Lord Ellery. I especially enjoyed the chapters I read last night in the parlor, regarding the royal houses of...Holt." She paused for emphasis, hoping he would follow. "Though one might *lift a brow* over the actions at the *hands of the kings and queens.*"

It had taken effort to spot the gestures that revealed Lord Holt's cards the previous evening. He was a careful one. At the table, he always sat with his back to the corner, ever watchful. Nevertheless, Gemma had discovered a few interesting tells.

As if perfectly attuned to her, understanding resonated in Sam's grin. "Your insight enthralls me. I should like nothing more than to hear all your thoughts, on any topic of your choosing."

She knew from the unreserved warmth of his tone they were no longer speaking of books or card play. And she tucked that knowledge away, keeping it close to her heart.

During the week, Gemma made a habit of visiting the library after dinner and picking up a different book before heading into the parlor with the others. What made this part of her day especially nice was that Sam did the same. In this way, her days were summed up in small moments in the library in the evening and then even smaller moments in the breakfast room each morning.

In the hopes of seeing him alone, Gemma had to rise earlier and earlier each morning. Sam seemed to be of like mind, for he was always standing near the door of the breakfast room, waiting for her with an expectant grin.

Then, invariably, one of the *four* would appear in a flurry of skirts, slippers scraping rapidly on the floor. Usually, this was Lady Cantham, who apparently took pleasure in wrinkling her nose at the buffet and making every attempt to command all of Sam's attention.

Nonetheless, just as he did during their not-so-private library trysts, he always found a way to be near Gemma.

Most often, he walked past her place at the table and paused to set a dish of something—marmalade, cream, or honey—in front of Gemma's plate. "Good morning, Miss Desmond," he said each time, the low timbre of his voice gliding through her and awakening her appetite. Bending beside her, his sleeve would brush her bare arm before he withdrew. And each time, he left her insides fluttering and tingling with longing.

She was desperate for an opportunity to be alone with him.

Yet the *four* were determined to keep them apart. They had split up into groups, making sure to trail either Gemma or Sam throughout each day. And Gemma often felt as if she were walking around wearing an archery target.

Thankfully, Sam hadn't been easily deterred. He'd found other ways of sharing private moments with her. Like on the day of horseback riding, when he walked over to her mount to ensure that she did not have a loose stirrup. His blunt fingertips grazed over the leather of her half boot as he secured her foot, leaving her with the briefest, most tantalizing touch above her ankle. There was also the afternoon in the village. While the others were buying new hair ribbons, she and Sam shared a single glass of Mrs. Selby's pink punch in the square.

And of course, there were the flowers.

For the past six nights when she retired to her bedchamber, she found a woodbine blossom on the window seat. And every night before she closed her eyes, she pressed her lips to the petals and placed it on the pillow beside hers.

After that first week, Gemma knew that no matter how the *four* interfered, it still did not detract from her growing feelings for Sam. Best of all—or worst of all; she still couldn't decide—she had an inkling that he felt the same way.

Today, she'd woken up with a terrifying truth. She was falling in love with him.

It left her torn. Sometimes Gemma forgot about her sullied surname and began to imagine a quiet life at Dunnock Park. Then other times, the *four* helped to remind her that she didn't belong here and that she should leave before something terrible happened that ruined Sam's good opinion of her.

"Did you hear me, my dear?" Aunt Edith asked from beside her as their party traipsed through the orchards and groves of Dunnock Park.

Gemma blinked, finding her way back to the present. She hoped her musings hadn't been transparent.

"I missed the last part," Gemma said, innocently owl-eyed.

Gradually, her previous thoughts dispersed and her surroundings became clear—the glossy green leaves covering branches heavy with ripe red fruits, and the crisp, mouthwatering scent of apples permeating the air.

"I said," Aunt Edith continued in a hushed voice, "that for the past week, I have not seen Lord Ellery without the company of Lady Tillmanshire, Lady Cantham, Miss Ashbury, Miss Leeds, or all of them together."

Gemma grumbled her displeasure. "We must allow them merits for diligence."

Directly ahead, the *four* took turns keeping him occupied by posing various questions.

"And what type of trees are these?" Miss Ashbury fairly shouted when Miss Stapleton had almost gained some of his attention.

"Apple," Sam said, his tone unusually terse.

Lady Tillmanshire issued a low, baying laugh that—to Gemma's ears—sounded eerily similar to the throaty growl of a cantankerous camel. "What an incorrigible flirt you are, Lord Ellery. Of course my daughter was asking for the Latin name."

"I'm afraid these apples do not speak Latin, my lady."

Another obnoxious laugh followed, and Sam cast a helpless glance over his shoulder to Gemma, rolling his eyes to the low-hanging canopy overhead. Gemma offered him a smile of support before he turned back to endure more inanity.

"Considering that the other gentlemen rode into town for a supposed surprise, Lord Ellery has been keeping us well entertained," Gemma said to her aunt. "I daresay there isn't a single woman who feels slighted by him."

"What about you? If he continues to divide his time between the others, then we will leave next week, and nothing will come of your acquaintance."

"Then it will be for the best." Gemma covered up the unexpected break in her throat with a cough.

"I do not believe that," Aunt Edith said, her mouth set in a stubborn line.

She sidled closer, not wanting to risk being overheard. "When my father is found, he will be tried for his numerous crimes, and his family will all have to endure the speculation and rumor again. I would not saddle Lord Ellery with such an ordeal to bear."

"Our host is not the type of man to care about your name or father's reputation. Why not present him with your concerns and allow him to choose the path he would take?"

"I cannot." She wasn't sure what scared her the most— what would happen if he chose her, or how desolate she would feel if he didn't.

Having reached their destination, the party stopped. Each group began unfolding the quilted blankets they carried as the footmen opened picnic baskets.

"I do not like how resigned you are, my dear," Aunt Edith said with quiet vehemence. Hooking the curved handle of her parasol over her forearm, she took hold of two corners. "You're waiting for the worst to happen instead of taking measures to ensure the best outcome."

Gemma gave the blanket a firm shake, settling her side on the ground. She waited until they were both seated in close proximity before speaking her mind. "Believe me, Aunt, if the choice were mine, I would order carriages for all the other women and send them away. Then I would lock out the rest of the world as well and live contentedly here at Dunnock Park."

There. She'd said it, the words so freeing that she could almost feel them taking flight, rising high above the walls she'd built around her heart.

Yet the truth of misguided confessions was that, eventually, they fell to their demise, much like Icarus and his wax wings.

"*All the other women?* Even me?" Aunt Edith sniffed with feigned despair. Her grin, however, gave her away. Clearly, she was pleased by her niece's admission.

Gemma pressed a kiss to her soft, lavender-scented cheek. "After plaguing me all afternoon, I daresay you might be the first to go."

Her aunt's lilting laugh drew attention from the others. Ellery's smile was automatic, and even Miss Stapleton and the Misses Creighton grinned. As expected, the *four* did not.

"It is such a lovely day that one cannot help but laugh with contentment," Aunt Edith said to the party. "What a shame, Lord Ellery, that the other gentlemen could not be here with us."

Standing off to the side, Sam directed the footmen to fill teacups with an apple tisane and deliver them to each guest, and then he turned a playful smirk on Aunt Edith. "If that is your way of trying to ferret out information regarding the surprise I have planned, it won't work, Your Grace."

A determined gleam sparked within in Aunt Edith's eyes. "Certainly you could tell us if we are to expect seeing your parents at this…event."

"Perhaps it is not an *event* at all," he said with a sly shrug, no doubt to pique everyone's curiosity. "However, I can tell you this much—my parents will not be in attendance." When a round of discontented rumbles met his declaration, he added, "I do expect them to join us for dinner one evening, quite soon."

Gemma felt the heat of his stare, as if he spoke the last part solely to her. Beside her, Aunt Edith drew in a quick breath as if she saw the same thing. Disconnecting her gaze from Sam's, Gemma glanced to the group to see if anyone else had noticed. The Misses Creighton and Miss Stapleton were blissfully unaware and chatting among themselves. But the *four* were scrutinizing her severely.

Suddenly, the orchard felt like an icehouse for all the glacial daggers being launched in her direction. Yet knowing that they only said hurtful things out of Sam's earshot, she knew she was safe from whatever insults they could sling at her. It gave her an opportunity to view the *four* with a more objective eye.

Quite honestly, she could appreciate the reason for the slant-eyed glares Miss Ashbury and Miss Leeds sent her way. Lord Ellery was a prime catch, after all. If the women were to brandish their claws over any man, it ought to be one who was worth the effort. And Sam most certainly was.

At the end of her assessment, Gemma realized that the *four* were all bluster and no bite. Here at Dunnock Park, under Sam's watch, they held no real power.

Then, just as soon as she'd finished the thought, she noted Lady Cantham eyeing her while tapping a closed fan against her chin. A shiver of foreboding trickled down Gemma's spine.

"What an interesting necklace you have, Miss Desmond," Lady Cantham said.

"Thank you, my lady," Gemma responded hesitantly. Why, exactly, after so many days of receiving silence, had she now earned this apparently cordial observation?

The young baroness slid a sideways look to her stepdaughter. Then Miss Leeds sat forward, the nostrils of her flat nose narrowing on a sniff. "You always wear a different piece of jewelry each day, Miss Desmond. I wonder, do you travel with a treasure chest, or do you…randomly pick up objects from wherever you are staying?"

This was the first time Miss Leeds had spoken directly to her as well. At least, where everyone could witness their exchange.

"I have a few pieces I've collected over the years. This coral necklace, in particular, was a gift from my aunt." Wary, her attention flitted to Sam, seeking comfort.

He smiled in reassurance, but that soon altered when his gaze dipped to where her fingers touched the necklace, and his eyes darkened, warming. Likely, he was recalling their outing on Leith Hill when Aunt Edith had beseeched him to assist with the clasp. And now she was too.

A sudden rush of heat stumbled through her, flushing her cheeks for all to see. Embarrassed, she reached for her cup and drank the cool tisane at the same time that Sam drained his own.

"I had a coral necklace, but I recently seem to have misplaced it," Miss Leeds said, her *s*'s rushing together in something of a hiss.

Gemma felt, rather than saw, Aunt Edith stiffen beside her. Several gazes were now on her coral necklace.

"But that is the problem with indistinct jewelry," Lady Tillmanshire interjected. "Take this cabochon ruby brooch, for instance, Lord Ellery. There isn't a single other one like it."

The moment Lady Tillmanshire gained his attention, she slid Gemma a sly glance, a malicious smile on her dromedary lips.

CHAPTER NINE

From the stables, Sam growled at the dark clouds rolling in to eclipse the red-tinted sunset. His guests were *supposed* to be busy later, enjoying a fireworks spectacle. But the coming storm had obliterated his plans for the evening.

Thankfully, Holt and Hollander *One* and *Two* had helped him gather up the fireworks display before they could get wet, while Lord Stapleton played host in Sam's absence. So at least there was a chance to see this through tomorrow. But waiting another night felt like an eternity.

"Well, that should just about do it," *One* announced from the outer corner of the empty horse stall. He released the crate early, nearly causing his younger twin to drop the other end, and dusted his hands together.

"Watch it, you!" *Two* shouted as he shuffled back, keeping his boot-clad feet out of harm's way.

The elder brother raked a careless hand over his widow's peak of sandy brown hair, ignoring the outburst, a wicked gleam in his jade green eyes. "I managed to pack up the fireworks and carry them back down the hill."

"Standing with your arms crossed, nitpicking the placement of every cylinder is hardly doing the work yourself," *Two* said, pantomiming with comical exaggeration, earning a tight-lipped sneer from his twin. "Additionally, I'm the one who carried the brunt of the weight since *your* arms are nothing more than spindly twigs beneath your shirtsleeves."

One absently brushed a piece of straw from shirtsleeves. "I am the elder brother, ergo the overseer."

"The quarter hour that separates us does not make you my lord and master."

"Of course not. Superiority in every other way does that for me."

Two's face split into a slow grin. "Well, at least I'm not the one who just stepped in horse shite."

The elder Hollander looked down and cursed.

With a shake of his head, Sam moved to the open doors where Holt was smoking a cheroot, his back resting against the weathered fieldstone wall. He took a long drag before flicking his ash in the water bucket at his feet.

"I suppose tonight will be cards again," Sam said without any interest. "I don't think I could stand another round of charades with Lady Tillmanshire and her shouting as if every puzzle were a horse race."

Holt chuckled. "I imagine it is a race to her. Rumor has it that the money her husband inherited—the same money that purchased his title and their home—is all but gone. Now, she is in desperate straits to find a well-situated husband for her daughter before anyone learns of their altered circumstances."

"Truly?" Sam wondered if that was the reason for their near frantic attempts to claim his attention. "Quite honestly,

I took pity on them. I thought that since they'd been labeled as *new money*, they were not being received properly within the *ton*. I wanted to give them a fair chance."

"A lesson for us all is to be wary of a woman in need of a fortune and a good name to save her," Holt said wryly. "Thankfully, I shall never have that problem. You, however, will have terrifying creatures to contend with until you finally marry."

Sam clenched his teeth and eyed his friend shrewdly. "I hope you are only referring to Lady Tillmanshire and Miss Ashbury with that comment."

"Of course. Who else would I—" Holt frowned, his cheroot paused midlift. "Ah. You thought I might also be referring to a certain Miss Desmond, whose 'surname is that of a criminal's.' It must be difficult to know that her father is very like the men who nearly took your father's life."

Sam's fists tightened. "Tread carefully, my friend. She is *not* like her father."

Unconsciously, his mind conjured an image of Gemma wearing a dark cloak, the lower half of her face hidden by a highwayman's scarf. A tormented shudder washed through him.

Quickly, he shook off the unsettling image. Gemma was no more of a thief and deceiver than he was, he assured himself.

Holt appraised him with an arched brow, then turned his attention to the sky. Drawing on his cheroot, he slowly released a thin, curling stream of smoke. "Does it bother you—her need of a good name to wipe the tarnish off her own?"

"No, what bothers me is the mean and unfounded censure she has endured."

"And as a result," Holt added, "she might assume that any offer of marriage she received would be out of sympathy and not realize you were already half in love with her."

Sam's fists relaxed in an instant. He drew in a deep breath sweetly scented with rain and tobacco. Like Gemma, Holt knew how to read people effectively. It was a trait Sam envied, now more than ever. "Yes, perhaps that too."

"And does she share your feelings?"

"You know very well that I've failed miserably in gauging a woman's interest before," Sam said, frustrated. "I would do better to ask you."

Holt flicked his ashes into the bucket. "While Miss Desmond looks at you as much you do her, she is rather cautious about revealing her thoughts in her expressions. So, from an outsider's perspective, it is difficult to tell. Though surely her kiss has told you all you need to know."

A sardonic laugh rumbled in Sam's throat. "That was the whole reason for the fireworks this evening."

He looked up to the house, a fireball sun reflected in the glass of Gemma's bedchamber window. Having her here, beneath his roof, should have made it much easier to spend time with her. And of course, he saw her far more frequently than he would have if they were in town. In their stolen moments, he'd come to know her better within the space of a week than he'd known any of the debutantes during the entire London Season.

Yet the problem was, he wanted to be alone with Gemma, talking without interruption, touching without the need to hide, and kissing without reason to stop.

He needed to know if he was foolishly risking his heart.

"You haven't kissed her yet? I've spent agonizing minutes in Lady Tillmanshire's and her daughter's company every night after dinner, solely to give you time alone in the library with Miss Desmond, and all for naught?"

"Perhaps if you'd told me of your plan to keep Lady Tillmanshire and her daughter occupied, we would not be having this discussion." Sam glared at his friend. "Besides, a man simply does not walk up to a woman and begin kissing her without a word."

"Not true. Some women happen to like that."

"Well, Gemma deserves more. She deserves respect and honor. From what I know of her life, she has seldom been asked what she would choose, and I would never forgive myself if I put my own desires above hers."

Though he had to confess, every moment he could get away with it, he touched her, stood close to her. She never once balked. In fact, she seemed receptive, enthrallingly so, her hand curling around his with the combined pleasure of new awareness and the ease of long-time intimacy. And that's exactly what he wanted—long, endless hours of intimacy. He was beginning to go mad with yearning. Even watching her from across the room—or a few blankets over in the apple orchard—and he'd become unbearably aroused.

"You are such a romantic," Holt said with combined pity and disgust. His cheroot dropped with a *sizzle* and a *plunk* as it hit the water. "Tell me, were you planning to embrace her beneath a shower of sparks for all your guests to see? Or were you naively hoping that no one would notice your absence while you wooed your possible bride-to-be?"

Sam swallowed. "The latter."

"And what? Were you going to trust the twins *not* to fire them off all at once and have the entire spectacle over in less than five minutes?" He clucked his tongue, looking over his shoulder to where *One* and *Two* were fencing with hayforks.

Hmm…that would pose a problem. "You have a point."

Holt faced him and clutched his shoulder. "We are going to need a grand production, my friend. Something to span at least…oh…thirty minutes. You need utter certainty, after all."

Until this moment, Sam never knew how indispensable a good friend could be.

CHAPTER TEN

The following evening, Gemma rushed through the garden. The firework spectacle was about to begin, and she didn't want to be late. Even more than that, she didn't want the party to be eaten by insects. Therefore, she needed to find lemongrass.

She'd seen it here, somewhere. Thankfully, with torches lit all around to mark the path down to the open park where everyone else was gathered, she had enough light to search. Now, if only her memory would guide her.

Trying to orient herself, she stopped for a moment only to discover that she was not the sole occupant of the garden. As luck would have it, the gardener she'd spied on a few occasions appeared through an arch near the hedgerow. Though, this was the first time during her stay that she'd seen him without his large straw hat and pruning shears.

He stopped on the path when he saw her, his blue eyes round until recognition creased them at the corners with his smile. "Why, Miss Desmond, shouldn't you be with the others, waiting eagerly for the firework spectacle?"

"You have no idea how happy I am to find you here," she said, feeling less anxious than before.

"You are not lost, are you?"

"Not exactly. I am in search of lemongrass. From what I understand, the scent deters biting insects, and after last night's rain, there promises to be a feast of human flesh unless we have some assistance. I know Lord Ellery wishes for everything to be perfect this evening."

He seemed to consider this, his head tilting in study of her. "And how do you know this?"

"Well, the truth of the matter is, I overheard him saying those words to Lord Holt only a few minutes ago. I sent my aunt with the rest of the party, promising to join her posthaste, but now I find myself wishing I could remember where I last saw the lemongrass."

"Right this way." With a knowing wink, he shuffled off the path, finding a narrow break between the slumbering foxglove and poppies. After a few steps they arrived at a small pebbled bird basin, surrounded by the lemongrass. Immediately, he withdrew his pruning tool from some unseen pocket and began to snip the fronds. "You are kind to think of everyone's comfort."

"It is only a kindness repaid to his lordship. He has selflessly ensured our enjoyment and even our contentment each day."

"He is a dutiful host."

"And the finest of men," she whispered, closing her hands over the offered bundle. Then, seeing the discerning expression on the gardener's face, she felt her cheeks grow hot. "I should go."

"If you had a ribbon in your hair or around your neck, I could tie those into fans for you."

"A fan! Oh dear, my aunt asked me to fetch one for her, and I forgot. She simply despises the scent of lemongrass, preferring to shoo away the insects instead." She peered over her shoulder to the house, wondering if she still had time.

The gardener took the fronds from her hands. "Go. I left a spool of twine under the bench beneath the arbor. I'll have these tied in proper bundles by the time you return."

"Thank you so very much." On impulse, she pressed a kiss to his papery cheek and then rushed back into the house.

Guided by the light from the sconce in the hall, Gemma went to her own chamber since it was closer than Aunt Edith's. Once inside, she walked toward the vanity where she kept her fan and grasped it before turning to leave. Yet when she spotted her jewelry box, she thought about the coral necklace.

Hmm… Sam looked at her rather warmly whenever she wore it, and she certainly wouldn't mind if he looked at her the same way this evening.

Making a quick decision, she placed the fan down and set her hand on the carved lid of the bleached wood box that stood on four shiny brass claws. A wealth of memories returned to her.

She'd been eleven years old when she'd first spotted it in a basket of wares in an Egyptian market, and she'd fallen instantly in love. Unfortunately, all she'd had were the few coins her father had given her to buy his snuff and her food. But given the fact that she'd had little guidance in money management up to that point—as her father always found a way to acquire whatever he wanted—she'd carelessly bartered away her entire fortune. She'd squandered every *para*, failing to gain a fair price because she hadn't concealed her desire for the box from the *tajir*.

As expected, her father had punished her. But not with a firm reprimand. He hadn't locked her in her room as he usually had, sent her to bed without supper, or even throttled her backside. No, instead he inflicted a far more severe and lasting penalty. He'd forced her to barter off every piece of her mother's jewelry.

Gemma had been six when her mother had died. The shape of her face, the sound of her laugh, and the scent of her hair had already begun to fade from Gemma's memory, leaving only faint traces behind. Those precious baubles had been the only things that were tangible, the only things that were left of her mother.

She remembered standing in the market that day, the heat of the sun bearing down on the scorched top of her head, drying the endless flow of tears on her cheeks. She'd wept pitifully, clutching each piece in her hand, refusing to sell because the people didn't understand that, to her, they were all priceless. No amount of money could take their place. But the offers only increased, and her father had been delighted to take their money.

When it was all over, and she was left with nothing but an empty jewelry box, her father had wiped away one tear from her cheek and held his glistening fingertip up for her study. "Now *this* is what makes something valuable. If you are selling, show them your reluctance to part with this precious trinket. And if you are buying, show them your indifference to it."

Indeed, Gemma had learned a valuable lesson—that a great number of people were inherently selfish. And she had to battle them all by herself.

Pushing those thoughts back into the past where they belonged, she lifted the lid to find her necklace. Then she frowned, momentarily confused. The few pieces she possessed were out of order. However, lying in the center was none other than Lady Tillmanshire's ruby brooch.

Gemma's heart slowed, and she stared at the crimson cluster for a beat or two, as if it were a deadly Buthridas scorpion. Then her pulse began to pound in her ears, her blood heating with anger as she realized what this meant.

The blasted *four* were trying to make Gemma out to be a thief.

Curling her hand over the cabochon gems, she felt the pin in the back prick her palm. Without waiting another moment, she strode out of her chamber, prepared to put it back in Lady Tillmanshire's room. But halfway down the hall, she paused.

What if Lady Tillmanshire had a maid waiting on her to do just that, waiting to catch her in the act? Gemma wouldn't put it past the conniving baroness.

The only way to avoid any consequence would be to return the brooch without her awareness. Perhaps a little sleight of hand would work. Gemma was out of practice, but she could find a way to slip it into the baroness's reticule. Better yet, she could pin the bloody thing on Lady Tillmanshire's frock— *then* let her try to accuse Gemma of stealing it.

Mind made up, Gemma stormed down the hall and toward the wide staircase.

Much to her surprise, she found Sam on his way up. They stopped simultaneously on the brocade runner, both out of breath. Though it was unlikely that Sam had an incriminating brooch burning the palm of his hand.

"There you are," he said, the corners of his eyes crinkling with his smile. "I was told you returned to fetch a fan. I just wanted to make sure you didn't get lost."

She glanced down at her empty hand, realizing she left the fan behind. Hesitating, she wondered if she should tell him about the brooch, or if it would be better to handle this matter on her own. But what if he didn't believe her claim?

She didn't think she could live with seeing doubt in his expression.

"I couldn't find it." She swallowed, tasting the lie at the back of her throat. "I thought it would be better to join the others as quickly as possible. I would not wish to miss the fireworks."

He held out his hand. "Then come, for I have a surprise for you."

Descending the stairs, she slipped her free hand into his and allowed the comfort of his grasp to ease some of her nerves.

Sam guided her down to the first floor, and while they walked along the corridor, she tried to tuck the brooch away. Unfortunately, she hadn't sewn pockets into her dress. Under her sash seemed too risky. It could fall and land with a clatter on the hardwood floors. Her only option was to slip it covertly into her bodice, securing the warmed metal between her breasts, low enough to be concealed and nestled firmly in her short stays. And she was just in time too, because Sam stopped suddenly at the end of the hall.

"I thought we might watch the fireworks from here," he said, opening one of a pair of double-arched doors leading to the ballroom. "That is...unless you'd prefer to join the others."

Inside was dark, absent of the golden sconce light in the hall. Through an expanse of crystal-clear mullioned windows, the beauty of the night sky was laid bare. And at the prospect of being alone with him, a jolt of anticipation zinged through Gemma, causing her hand to squeeze his tightly. "I'd like to stay."

"I'm glad," he said, pleasure warming his voice as he pulled her closer, leading her deeper into the room. "I took the liberty of sending the bundles of lemongrass you made down to the others with a footman."

Oh! It was awful of her, but she'd completely forgotten about the others. "The bundles weren't solely my idea. I offer the credit to your clever and thoughtful gardener."

"My *gard*—" He gave her a quizzical glance. Then he issued a sound that was something of a laugh. "Oh, yes. My gardener is invaluable to me."

Stopping when they reached the windows, she watched as several footmen, below, were snuffing out the torches one by one. "He is quite fond of you as well. Then again, I believe all your servants are."

"Most men, I imagine, wish to earn the regard of those *not* in their employ," he said wryly.

"You have that as well, and no doubt in abundance." Playfully, she nudged him with her shoulder. Yet by the time she felt the puffed sleeve of her lutestring dress crumple against her skin and connect with the firmness of his arm, she realized her error. If holding hands caused her pulse to riot, then she should have known that pressing another part—any part—of her body against him would have a similar if not substantially greater response.

Instantly, she bloomed with heat, their contact lighting a firework inside her. At the same time, the thick muscles of his arm bunched and a breath staggered out of him.

"How can you be certain?" he asked, his voice an intimate murmur.

It sent a shiver through her. "Well, I know my aunt is fond of you."

He angled toward her, his boots shifting to the outer edges of her slippers. The lapels of his coat were only a breath away from the rise and fall of her breasts. Lifting his hand to her cheek, his fingers glided along the slope of her jaw to her chin and tilted her face up to his. "And what of her niece?" The rapid beat of her heart made it difficult to release a breath. It was locked inside of her like so many recent hopes and dreams. Her lips tingled, plumping under his dark, searching scrutiny. And when the tip of her tongue darted out to wet them, his head dipped toward hers, close enough that she caught the clean, spicy scent of his shaving soap and felt the heat of his breath.

Her eyes drifted shut of their own volition. "I have it under good authority that she likes you. Very much, indeed."

His other hand released hers, his fingertips skimming up the length of her bare arm, setting off a shower of tingles. Cupping her face, he drew closer, his nose nuzzling beside hers. His lips brushed one corner of her mouth and then the other. "Enough to permit me to kiss her?"

A soft laugh escaped her. "I believe you already are."

And it was heaven, these slow, searching nibbles at her lips, the feel of his warm breath against her skin.

"Not yet," he said with more sampling tastes of the corners of her mouth and a sly sweep along the center. Cradling her face in his hands, he went still, waiting for her answer.

Restraint emanated from him in the small vibrations through his fingertips and in each shuddered breath between her parted lips. He would take only what she was willing to give. He was not selfish. His honor and decency were not merely for show. These qualities were part of him and in his every action.

And she loved him all the more for it.

But this was not the time for hesitation. They'd been patient for long enough. *Ages and ages.* She wanted him to know that he didn't need to hold back. Not with her.

Slanting her head, she whispered against his lips, "Then show me."

On a low groan, he dragged his mouth across hers. The hot, firm pressure caused pleasure sparks to explode behind her eyelids, and she melted against him, feeling the faint rasp of his whiskers. A series of wanton tingles spiraled through her body and shuddered out of her throat.

"Do you like that?" His heavy breath brought the rich, earthy flavor of him into her mouth, his tongue skating across the plump, sensitive inner swell of her bottom lip. Then, nudging her lips apart, he fed his tongue to her in small sips, easing himself deeper into the warmth of her mouth. "And this?"

She couldn't speak but only emitted inarticulate mews of pleasure. He swallowed them down in ravenous open-mouthed kisses. Long, scorching kisses that incinerated any vestige of hesitancy or uncertainty. Wanting more, she slipped inside his coat and splayed her hands over the cashmere of his waistcoat as she rose up on her toes.

His hold on her shifted, one hand sliding to the back of her neck, the other at her waist, her hip. Then, fitting into the curve of her lower back, he hitched her up against the solid length of him. Delicious tremors tumbled through her. There was a sense of inevitability in the gesture, a promise that this was only the beginning.

He slowed his assault, his tongue gliding over hers as deep rumbles of pleasure rippled from his throat. Somehow she knew their kiss would be like this—a hot torrent one minute, a languid savoring the next—as if they were both saying *At last*, and *I need you now*, but also *Let's not rush* and *Don't ever stop*.

Outside, she could hear the distant pops and crackles of the spectacle, but she wasn't missing anything. Inside, she was on fire, burning for him. His teeth nipped her bottom lip and her stomach clenched so tightly—so sweetly—that she gasped and pulled herself closer, her hips tilting to fit against his.

A stab of pleasure bolted through her, causing another sound to escape, this one throaty, greedy, and foreign to her own ears. But Sam seemed to recognize it, for his hand slipped down to the curve of her derriere, drawing her tightly against him. And when he rolled his hips forward, her knees went weak.

"My legs are trembling," she said when his mouth left hers, and his damp lips grazed the underside of her jaw in a way that made her entire body clench with untried desire.

He pressed kisses along her throat, his arms locked around her. "I have you. *Mmm*...you smell as sweet as woodbine here."

His ardent attentions only made her problem worse. Now her entire body was trembling uncontrollably.

"Put your arms around me." Then he turned her, moving them a few steps along the floor in something of a slow, sensuous dance until the wall was at her back, cool against her bare shoulder blades, while he was pressed along her front, hotter than ever. "Is this better?"

She blushed but nodded, her hands sliding through the cool tips of his soft golden curls to the heat of his scalp. Boldly, she pulled him closer and slanted her mouth beneath his. His lips were well suited for kissing, even more than for smiling and laughing. It was easy—effortless—to lose herself against their broad shape.

In his arms, she began to hope that she could have the life she'd only dared to imagine in her dreams. With a good, solid man to love her as much as she loved him.

She breathed his name, her head falling back as he blazed a new path down her throat, dipping his tongue into the hollow notch.

He groaned against her skin. "You taste like nectar and rain. Somehow, I knew you would. And your skin"—he lifted his head to watch the unhurried progress of his fingertips follow the line of her bodice over her rapidly rising and falling breasts—"your skin is softer than petals."

Her whole body clenched again, her breasts drawing taut, her nipples newly sensitive beneath her chemise. "And did you know that too?"

"Aye." He grinned at her and then kissed her again, his hands skimming down the outer swells and settling into the warmth beneath. His long fingers curved around her rib cage while his thumbs swept tantalizingly, back and forth, against the plump underside of her breasts.

Sam's gaze was hungry, tender, and drowsy all at once. He looked from her face down to her bodice and to the pebbled tips of her nipples outlined against the layers of cambric and blue muslin. They were nearly painfully taut and heavy. As if he sensed this, he slid his hands higher to assuage the ache, molding them around her breasts, his thumbs rasping over the peaks.

"Sam," she said, choking with a need she didn't know how to name. Reflexively, she arched her back, filling his hands. Her lips parted to gasp, to moan, but pleasure clogged her throat, and all she could do was feel those tight buds growing even tighter until she thought she might go mad. "Please…"

He dipped his head, pressing his mouth to the top of the plump globe of flesh. But it was not enough. He continued to press kisses all along the line of her bodice, increasing the ache until it spread throughout her body, seating itself in a tense, throbbing sensation at the apex of her thighs. Dragging the edge of her sleeves down her shoulders, he drew down the fabric, and exposed her flesh to the balmy night air, inch by inch.

And then the worst thing that could possibly happen, happened.

She'd forgotten about the brooch.

CHAPTER ELEVEN

It took Sam a moment to realize that something was amiss. He was still deep in a haze of lust and staring at the most beautiful breasts he'd ever seen. They were pale and perfect with ruched, dusky peaks.

Then, suddenly, they were gone, wrenched out of his sight in a flurry as Gemma turned away, her gaze lowered to the floor.

Only vaguely had he heard something fall. Now he looked down as well, trying not to pay attention to the thick, throbbing erection straining against the fall of his breeches. The task proved to be quite difficult. He still had the sweet taste of her skin on his tongue and her lush scent filling his nostrils, permeating every breath. His hands were still tingling, imprinted with the softness of her flesh, and his entire body pulsed with the desire to hold her against him again.

Without conscious thought, he took a step toward her but then paused when he caught sight of the object on the floor.

Strange. "That's Lady Tillmanshire's brooch. I recall seeing it at the picnic," he said, carefully bending to pick it up. "Gemma, why do you have it?"

Her shoulders stiffened, the movements of her hands briefly stalled in the process of setting her sleeve aright. Then, after clearing her throat, she finished and turned to face him.

Her lips were red and swollen from his kiss, her cheeks still flushed. She swallowed, her gaze darting from his face to the brooch in his hand. "You automatically believe me capable of stealing it?"

Actually, that hadn't occurred to him…until now. Suddenly, Holt's words from just a day ago resurfaced. *It must be difficult to know that her father is very like the men who nearly took your father's life.*

In Gemma's eyes, Sam glimpsed what he thought was a shadow of hurt. But could it have been guilt instead? "It was in your possession, and I do not know what to think."

Two voices were at war inside him. The one in his heart told him that Gemma was not a thief simply because her father was. Then his head reminded him that he'd known her for less than a fortnight. How could any man know a person's character in such a short time?

Gemma lifted her chin, her throat tight. "I found it in my bedchamber a few moments ago, and I was going to return it."

"But that doesn't make sense," he said, logic winning over feeling. "The baroness would not have mistaken your bedchamber for her own, and neither would her maid."

"Correct."

Sam waited for her to say more, to offer something of an explanation. Instead, she simply stared at him with that unnamed emotion roiling in the depths of her green-blue eyes.

So he tried to put the pieces together on his own.

"You found the brooch and decided to return it directly," he said carefully. "And that was when I encountered you on the stairs…leaving the second floor with Lady Tillmanshire's brooch tucked inside your clothing."

"In truth, it was in my hand at the time. I only managed to slip it inside my bodice while you and I were walking to this room."

He frowned. There it was—that striking frankness of hers. And yet it did her no favors. She'd just admitted to purposely concealing the brooch from him, which left him with a renewed sense of doubt and dread.

"Was this the reason you kissed me, to conceal it?" He didn't intend to ask the question—especially not with so much bitterness in his tone—but now that it was between them, he wanted to know the answer.

Nothing had ever felt so right as having Gemma in his arms. In those moments, he'd had no reason to question her regard. The uncertainty that had plagued him suddenly evaporated in the heat of her passionate response.

Now, however, with the brooch between them, he wondered if he'd been blinded by his own desires, unable to see the truth. Yet again.

She flinched, then quickly averted her eyes. "I thought you wanted me to be exactly who I am."

"Yes. And I thought that person was honest and true. Tell me I was not wrong."

When she did not answer, his hands curled around the brooch in frustration, his fist falling to his side. Then the rumbles of excited chatter drifted upward from below stairs.

Combined with laughter, the sound was dissonant, pinging like hailstones on glass during a fierce storm.

The last thing he wanted in this moment was for his guests to return. But they had, nonetheless.

"We cannot be discovered alone," he said. For the sake of her already fragile reputation, he would not reveal any of the events that had transpired. "We will continue this discussion in the morning. In the meantime, should the other guests comment on your absence, I will say that you had taken ill to avoid any…repercussions. Are you amenable to that?"

Turned away, her face in profile, she offered a crisp nod.

Unable to linger a moment longer, he strode out of the room, intent on returning the brooch to Lady Tillmanshire's chamber without anyone the wiser.

Gemma had no trouble pretending to be ill. The last words exchanged between her and Sam left her raw and cold from her skin to the marrow of her soul. The shivers that stole over her seemed to settle in her stomach, freezing her until she felt brittle all over.

He thought she was a thief.

It turned out that his opinion of her was no better than anyone else in society. They all assumed she was capable of terrible things, just like her father. She'd been a fool to hope otherwise.

The fear that she would never escape Albert Desmond's influence over her life had come to fruition.

As she packed a satchel, she held back an incipient sob with short, strangled breaths that burned her throat. Then, desolate, she slipped down the narrow servant's staircase and eventually found herself outside, in the garden. She planned to go to the inn at Banfern Glenn and, at first light, she would send a note to her aunt.

Surely by then the news of her supposed theft would have spread throughout the house. They would need to leave immediately to flee the tidal wave of rumors that was soon to strike. Perhaps if they set off for North's country estate or even one of Cousin Liam's houses toward the north of England, somehow they might escape the worst of it.

But when the truth hit her, Gemma stopped, her slippers scraping to a halt on the stone path beneath the rose arbor.

There was *no* escaping it. She would be ostracized, and her family along with her. The irrefutable fact broke over her in a wave of hopelessness. Collapsing on the bench beneath the arbor, she slumped forward, expecting the sob to wrench free. But it didn't. It was trapped inside her, chafing the raw interior of her lungs and blistering her throat.

Why wouldn't it just leave in one cathartic release? Then she could be done with it.

Still, it stayed with her, taunting her, and reminding her of the misery she'd brought to her family.

Growing up, moving from place to place, living with a man who spewed deception and manipulation from every pore, she'd been so lonely. All she'd wanted was to return to her aunt and her cousins, to love them, to start living a normal life, and perhaps to find a measure of contentment along the way. Yet even after returning to London, she hadn't truly believed it was possible. Not until she met Sam.

With him, the world seemed different, brighter. Oh, she knew well enough that there would always be darkness lurking around the corner. Yet she'd realized there could also be places where she felt safe. Where she could be herself without fear of judgment. Sam had helped her see that. And she liked this altered perspective, this fresher, hopeful version of herself. She liked who she was when she was with him.

She opened her mouth in silent, frustrated agony, thinking of how she would never be with him again. Shoulders shaking in defeat, she buried her face in her hands.

"What's the matter, child?"

She jerked upright, dry-eyed, to see the gardener's troubled expression. When he laid a hand on her shoulder, a miserable, keening sound slipped out of her throat, and she was helpless to hold it back.

"It is n-nothing. I w-was just g-going for a stroll, and something fell into my eyes." She turned away and pressed a hand to her eyes, hating herself even for this small deception.

"That happens from time to time"—he reached forward and presented a folded handkerchief—"especially during night walks, when you're carrying a satchel. When your hands are full, it leaves you without a way to shield your eyes."

Looking askance at him, there was no way to miss the knowing arch of his brows, or the blue eyes that seemed to possess the power to look right through her. She knew he was going to ask why the packed satchel was on the ground beside her feet. And if she gave him the reasons she had to leave, undoubtedly he would offer some wisdom about how worries tend to vanish by morning.

But that would not be true in her circumstance. Things were only going to get worse.

Clutching his handkerchief in her hand, she shook her head and went directly to the point of the matter. "I cannot go back."

Much to her surprise, he didn't dispute her. Instead, he nodded sagely and made himself comfortable on the bench beside her.

Long moments stretched on for an eternity, and all he did was sit there with his hands clasped in his lap, and his head titled back to breathe in the warm night air that was turning thick with the scent of coming rain. His patience was almost diabolical.

It only took about one minute—an embarrassingly short time—before she cracked. The reserved demeanor that had been second nature to her for most of her life was nowhere to be found.

A slow but steady trickle of tears seeped out from one eye and then the next. Then all her thoughts and feelings came flooding out in one jumbled mess. She was sure she wasn't even making sense, just blubbering and going on and on about her father, the wicked *four horsewomen*, the planted brooch, and then Sam. "And his face...I'll never forget how hurt and betrayed he looked. He actually thought that I...kissed him to conceal a crime. It hurt me so deeply that I was speechless." She found the only dry corner of the handkerchief and blew her nose in it. "I could have endured anything if only he'd trusted me."

Somewhere, during the course of her utter humiliation, the gardener had settled an arm around her shoulders and let

her rest her head against him. "Now I'm beginning to understand why you are out here. Though I'm sorrier than you can
imagine if he made you feel as if you had to leave. Especially
in the middle of the night."

"No, that decision was my own. Throughout all of it, Lord
Ellery remained courteous, never cruel." That was something
she loved about him. No matter what he might have thought
of her, he still treated her kindly. "But seeing his doubt
destroyed any hope I had."

"Hmm…I wonder if it was not doubt but something else
instead," the gardener mused, patting her shoulder. "Perhaps it was the topic of thievery that gave his countenance a
troubled appearance. You see, little more than a year ago, his
father was attacked by highwaymen and robbed. He might
have been killed as well if he hadn't collapsed on the side of
the road from a heart seizure and saved them the trouble.
They left him for dead, all the same."

She gasped, her own worries forgotten. "Oh, I had no
idea. How dreadful! His father…is he still alive?"

"Yes, but his health is…well, not what it once was."

She looked out across the drowsy garden, thinking of how
difficult it must have been for Sam to allow her to stay after
she'd told him about her own thieving father. And yet, Sam
had never once given her the feeling of not being welcome here.

"And through my own stubbornness, I let Sam assume
that I was guilty," she said, crestfallen. "If I'd only known
this, then I would go back to that moment and…" She shook
her head. "But no. It is too late. If I were to speak to him
now, it would seem as if I'd spent all this time fabricating a
story to redeem myself. Besides, there would be no point in it.

Nothing can alter the fact that Albert Desmond's daughter has no place here. It's better that I go, for everyone's sake."

"What of those four women?" The gardener blustered, sitting up straighter and gesturing toward the house. "Are you just going to let them run roughshod over him, convincing him that they are perfectly suited as his bride, and then doom him to a life of misery?"

She looked toward the house too, worried. "He's far too intelligent to be fooled by their true natures."

"And yet he invited them."

"See here," she scolded, not liking his skeptical tone. "Lord Ellery is above and beyond the most excellent man I have ever known. His deeply rooted goodness touches everyone he encounters. He deserves to be praised for his good opinion of others, not ridiculed."

The gardener looked at her, a slow smile spreading across his face, lifting his cheeks to the outer corners of his bushy, arched brows. "You sound as if you love him."

What an impertinent gardener!

"Anyone who knows him would feel the same." She stood and took hold of her satchel, prepared to leave in a huff. Then his next words stopped her midstep.

"His mother and I have always thought so too."

Gemma's foot settled slowly back down onto the path. *His mother and...*

She swallowed. *Oh, please don't let it be true.* It was one thing to embarrass oneself in front of a gardener but quite another to do so in front of the father of the man you loved.

She couldn't even turn around to face him. She squeezed her eyes shut. "You mean to say that you're his..."

"Father," he supplied gently. "Edwin Wortham, the Marquess of Russford. It is a pleasure to make your acquaintance, Miss Desmond."

Eventually, she turned around, thinking she couldn't embarrass herself any more than she already had. Then, of course, she did.

While dipping into a curtsy, she suddenly remembered that she'd confessed *everything*, even the part about kissing Sam—and then she stepped on her own hem and stumbled forward.

"*Oh, drat!*" Somehow, she managed to stop midlurch before she collided with him. "Please forgive me for my outburst, Lord Russford. *All* of them. It seems that I am meant to make a disaster out of this entire day."

The marquess laughed softly. "Think nothing of it. We all find ourselves tangled up in situations, either of our making or someone else's, from time to time. But, if I may be so bold, I should like to ask what you plan to do about yours?"

And then, because the day wasn't through with her yet, more tears sprang to her eyes, and she began to blubber all over again. "I don't have the faintest idea."

CHAPTER TWELVE

Just past sunrise the following morning, Sam paced his study, waiting for Gemma.

He'd lain awake all night thinking about the events that had transpired, all the things that Gemma had said, and all the things she hadn't. After mulling it over for endless hours, he still couldn't reconcile why the brooch had been in her possession.

He knew she wasn't a thief. He'd had a sense of her character from that very first day and every moment since. Someone so honest that she couldn't deceive a fish would never have taken what didn't belong to her. And someone so direct would have told him right off if she had. So there had to be another explanation.

Given the circumstances at that time, however, he hadn't been clear-headed enough to settle the matter before they parted. And for him, the morning hours couldn't come soon enough.

"Beg pardon, m'lord," Mrs. Harkens said, clasping her perpetually reddened hands, her faintly lined countenance troubled. "Miss Desmond was not in her chamber."

The news was not wholly unexpected. Considering the events of last night, Gemma might have sought comfort from her aunt. Although, thinking of her feeling frail and knowing he was at least partly to blame turned like cold porridge in his stomach. "Then she is likely with the dowager duchess. Perhaps you might—"

Before he could finish, the housekeeper was already shaking her head, setting free the wiry strands of graying hair from her cap. "I thought as much, but when I peered inside Her Grace's chamber, Miss Desmond wasn't there either. Their maid, Berta, knew nothing of it, and when she checked Miss Desmond's chamber, she noticed that her satchel and several items of clothing were missing from the wardrobe." She hesitated before continuing. "It appears she's gone, m'lord."

Gone? No. That couldn't be. Surely Gemma wouldn't have run away, believing that he would allow her to be accused of thievery. He'd placed the brooch back in Lady Tillmanshire's room himself. Moreover, he'd told her they'd finish their discussion in the morning, so she knew he expected to see her. *She couldn't have run away.*

Then he remembered what she'd said that first day in the garden when she was ready to leave.

"The very name I hold is a black mark against my entire family. And I cannot in good conscience tarnish your household with my presence."

"Because of my presence at Dunnock Park, your own very good name may fall under scrutiny."

Suddenly, he knew it was true. Gemma was gone.

Alarm rushed through him in an avalanche of shockwaves that left him staggered. He gripped the edge of his desk for support.

"Send word to the stables to saddle my horse," he said, thinking that the next likely place for her was the inn at Banfern Glenn. He only hoped he would find her there, hoped that he would find her at all.

Dread climbed up his throat and tasted bitter on his tongue. If anything happened to her, he would be lost. He couldn't waste another instant. So before Mrs. Harkens could leave, he stopped her. "Never mind. I'll go there myself. In the meantime, please see to Her Grace's comfort and try to keep this matter as quiet as possible."

He strode through the house and went out the back entrance, through the garden. Fueled by dire thoughts, he didn't even see the aged footman turning the corner at the hedgerow until they'd nearly collided.

"Forgive me, my lord," Abney said, hunching his shoulders forward to protect the silver salver he carried. Unfortunately, the folded letter he carried fell to the ground anyway.

Preoccupied, Sam bent to retrieve it, only listening with half an ear as Abney continued.

"Didn't expect to see anyone else up and about. Lord Russford asked me to take this missive to the Dowager Duchess of Vale straightaway. Urgent matter and all that."

"Yes, of course. No apologies necessary. The fault was"— Sam hesitated before handing over the letter—"mine."

He looked at the handwriting closely, not recognizing the loopy slanted scrawl. His mother's handwriting was far more ornate, with superfluous vine-like additions to every letter.

His father's was a tall, slender script that went straight up and down.

Sam looked intently at Abney. "Who sent this?"

"A recent guest at the dower house, a Miss Desburn—something or other."

"Desmond?" Even as Sam asked the question, he already knew the answer.

His gaze moved past the footman to the whitewashed façade of the dower house. His heart continued to thud rapidly beneath his chest. But instead of feeling dread in every heavy beat, he felt a mixture of relief...and anger. Coupled together, the two emotions did not sit well with him and the sickening worry she'd caused.

Sending Abney on his errand, Sam strode out of the garden and straight through the front door of the cottage. When he finally saw Gemma, he wasn't sure if he would throttle her or kiss her.

Gemma stepped into the cozy solarium to find Sam's mother busy at her needlework, her spectacles perched low on her nose and a thick plait of her buttery blonde and ash gray hair draped over the shoulder of her blue morning gown. She sat an angle from the bank of windows behind her, letting the light fall over the wide quilting stand in front of her.

Miriam Wortham, the Marchioness of Russford, glanced up and offered a warm smile. "Good morning, dear. Were you able to sleep at all?"

Gemma shook her head. There was no point in trying to hide it. She'd learned from her reflection that she looked a fright, with purplish bruises beneath her eyes, pale cheeks, and a red nose. "I want to apologize again, Lady Russford, for disturbing your own sleep."

"Nonsense. As I said before, Mr. Wortham and I only nap a few hours each night. You disturbed nothing but a few backaches and leg cramps, and for that I should thank you." She patted her hand on the arm of the upholstered chair beside hers. "Now, come and sit here, and let the sunlight cheer you."

Like her son, she was overwhelmingly generous and kind. She'd even gone out of her way to go to the kitchens and prepare a cup of hot milk with honey for Gemma not long after she'd arrived. Lady Russford had not pressed her with any questions but likely had heard the bulk of Gemma's problems when she'd spoken to her husband. And even though Gemma felt guilty for trespassing on their hospitality, it was also a relief to be among them.

Sam's parents—who called each other *Mr.* and *Mrs. Wortham* with great affection—possessed the calming serenity of two people who lived in perfect harmony with each other. They were considerate and loving, not only to one another but also to their servants and even to the weeping stranger who had burst unceremoniously into their lives. It was impossible not to feel more at ease here.

Yet as Gemma sat, she had to turn away from the view of the gardens that led to the manor house. It was still too difficult to think of Sam. To think of never seeing him again.

She stifled a forlorn sigh. "I sent a missive to my aunt a few moments ago. I'm sure it will only be a matter of time before we leave Dunnock Park."

"I know that is your plan, but I still wish you would reconsider. If nothing else, you and the dowager duchess are welcome to stay here. I should like the company and, if either of you were so inclined, a needlework partner to help me finish this counterpane in time," she said with a small, effortless smile.

"It is extraordinarily beautiful," Gemma said, not wanting to make a new argument about how she would only sully their names for aiding her. Instead, she touched the deep blue silk of the counterpane, admiring the flawless stitches and the beautiful mixture of threads in dark umber, forest green, and silvery white, forming embroidered vines that climbed over the outer edges. The bottom of the counterpane was a layer of the finest wool, the center filled with the softest down. "If I may inquire, why the rush for its completion?"

"This is my Samuel's wedding quilt."

Gemma's hand tightened reflexively over the edge of heavy silk. Then, realizing what she'd done, she quickly released it and pressed her tingling fingertips against her lips in case a renewed sob should suddenly rise up her throat. She didn't want to think about him marrying and lying beneath this counterpane with his bride, kissing someone else and touching her the way he'd kissed and touched Gemma last night.

Thankfully, the sudden searing jealousy brought on by that thought kept her from crying, and she eased her hand down to her lap. "I was under the impression that he had yet to decide, that he was patient and…and cautious."

Then again, likely he wanted to make a quick decision in order to cut any lingering ties with the supposed thief in his midst.

"Ah, to be sure," Lady Russford answered with a sigh as she worked the end of a fresh spool of thread through her needle. "Though he's not had any luck with it. You would not think it to know him, but he was cast aside by the woman he'd thought to wed, and another still whom he'd thought of courting. Both of them surprised him with the news that they loved another."

In Gemma's opinion, any woman who did not choose Sam over another man was daft indeed. "You are correct, for I could never imagine such a thing."

"He certainly wasn't expecting it, and ever since, he's lost faith in his own judgment." Lady Russford clucked her tongue. "He had a plan, you see. He knew that if he carefully considered all the debutantes and found someone who shared his interests and possessed a similar disposition, then he would find his ideal bride. Of course, I told him all along that he was forcing his own regard to be greater than it was. He never thought once about what his heart might prefer. And the heart always knows, wouldn't you agree?"

Gemma swallowed. "Some might say that it's a difficult organ to trust."

"Some might," the marchioness said, her clear blue eyes peering over the brass rims of her spectacles and offering an encouraging grin before she returned to plying her needle. "I suppose it's easy to take the heart for granted. We hardly need to think about its beating for us, all day and night, day after day, year after year. Instead, we tend to think about it only when it breaks. But a broken heart is only one stitch in a long row, is it not? If this counterpane had only one stitch, it would be weak indeed; however, there are rows upon rows, each one making the next stronger and more lasting."

Tentatively, Gemma traced one of the rows nearest her, wishing that reality were as simple as Lady Russford made it sound. She could already feel her heart breaking, and it seemed to span much more than one single stitch. She suspected that it would fray every beat of her heart for the rest of her life.

At the sound of footsteps in the corridor, her gaze shifted to the doorway in time to see the marquess appear. Then, before Gemma could steel herself, Sam was there too.

"Mrs. Wortham, look who came to visit us, bright and early," Lord Russford said with a smile as he patted his son's shoulder.

But Sam did not smile. His jaw was set, his posture stiff, his eyes a hard glacier blue as they swept over Gemma. Briefly, his gaze shifted away. "Good morning, Mother."

"And to you, dearest," she said cheerfully. "Miss Desmond was just helping me with your wedding present."

Snapping back to Gemma, his expression grew darker, a muscle flicking with irritation along his jaw. "How convenient that she should be *here* to assist you, instead of at the manor house, where she was expected to be."

Gemma stood, needing distance from the wedding blanket, and also to rally her own defenses. "Your parents were good enough to invite me to stay, and I am ever so grateful for it."

"Yes. I suppose it is *good enough* that you are here. That you are not in Banfern Glenn, unchaperoned. Or lying in a ditch somewhere along the way, bloodied and broken. Or worse." Tension rolled off him in waves, seeming to disturb the air surrounding him, shimmering in the way the sun does to the searing desert horizon. He took two hard strides into the room toward her, his fists clenched at his sides. "Yes, that is *good enough*. I am well pleased by this happy turn of events."

"Samuel," his father scolded, "mind your tone. The girl was beside herself last night."

Sam looked her up and down, a flash of something other than fury heating his gaze before he blinked, and it disappeared. "She seems to have recovered."

"I wish the same could be said of you. I do not know what has gotten into you." Lady Russford stood, a frown pulling at her pale brows and lips. "You are certainly not offering an accurate representation of how you were raised to behave."

Gemma looked to her hostess. "The fault is mine, my lady. I see now that I should have left a note." Then she faced Sam. "I did not think you would notice my absence before my aunt had the opportunity to inform you of it."

"A *note?*" Sam said with a hollow, incredulous laugh.

Gemma didn't know how to respond. He was far more upset than she could have suspected.

"Mrs. Wortham, let us go to the breakfast room and let Samuel sort out this matter," the marquess said, holding out his hand for his wife. "Miss Desmond, should you require anything, we shall be just down the hall."

She offered a nod, feeling a knot twisting inside her as she turned back to Sam. In all the years of studying other people, she had not witnessed this particular expression and wasn't sure what it meant.

"I never intended to anger you with my absence," Gemma said once they were alone, hesitant to take a step toward him.

"I'm not angry. Not really." He expelled a hard breath, then pinned her with his stare. "Gemma, if our situations were reversed, and you expected to find me safe and exactly where I was supposed to be but then discovered that I had gone without leaving word, would that worry you?"

The very thought of it caused a cold chill to sweep through her. "Well, of course. I would be beside my—*oh*." She understood now that it wasn't fury he was feeling but concern. And perhaps, even more than that. Though she dared not think what it could mean without fear of feeding a fruitless hope.

She shuffled a half step closer, finding comfort in his nearness, even with the tangible barrier between them. "I apologize for leaving without a word. It was thoughtless of me."

This time, he released a slower breath, his shoulders relaxing. "No. I'm the one who should apologize. I've behaved beastly this morning. I've only experienced this sense of all-consuming panic once before, and I do not know how to reconcile myself with it."

Gemma guessed the answer in an instant. "Was it when your father was attacked by highwaymen?"

"Yes," he said, his expression curious. "How did you know?"

"His lordship told me of it last night when he found me in the garden. In that same instant, I knew how terrible it was of me to let you believe that I'd stolen the brooch," she confessed, and she noticed that his hands were no longer fisted at his side. Seeing those long, capable fingers and that broad palm made her hand feel empty. So she rolled her fingers

inward and tried not to think about it. "Given the circumstances of my life, I wasn't sure you'd trust me to tell you the
truth. Regardless, I want you to know now that I would never
steal. And if I wanted to exact revenge on Lady Tillmanshire,
I would be far cleverer."

His mouth twitched in something of a grin. "I have no
doubt of it." Then, when he took a step closer, a tremble of
longing coursed through her. "Gemma, I do not think you
took the brooch. If you say it was put there by accident—"

"It was no accident," she said again, feeling the sting of her
own temper.

"—then I believe you."

Those words, said with such conviction, caused her breath
to hitch. That strange, lopsided whirring started spiraling
inside her lungs once more. Lifting her face, she studied him
closely, wanting to believe it could be true. "But last night I
did not think you were so certain."

"I confess that I was surprised. And though it is no excuse,
my mind was not quick to process the alteration from a most
pleasant series of events"—his gaze drifted to her lips—"to
their sudden turn."

"I was taken off guard as well."

At the memory, her cheeks grew hot. How could it be that
even hours later she could still feel his kiss, and his mouth
on her throat as if he'd branded her? She felt tingly, aware of
every pulse point and the small distance between them.

Sam shifted closer and lifted his hand to her face. As
soon as he touched her, the air inside the solarium seemed to
simmer, thawing the frozen, desolate parts of her in a rush.
His thumb swept across her lower lip. A jolt of pleasure sank

deep, deep down into her center, causing something inside of her to clench sweetly.

Then he cradled her face between both his hands, his eyes dark and intent. Bending his head, he grazed his lips over hers, drawing out a whimper of longing from her throat.

"You like that," he said without question, pressing nibbling kisses against the corners of her mouth. "You're trembling."

Lifting her hands, she encircled his wrists, feeling the strength of him in the sinew, bone, and the blood coursing beneath her fingertips. She pressed her lips to his, seeking, wanting.

When he took her mouth, it was as if they'd never been apart, with nothing—no brooch, no doubt—between them. He tilted her head back, the sensuous slide of his tongue over hers obliterating all thought. She was a taut bundle of need and desire, feeding on each deep, searing kiss as if it were their last.

She was struck by the sense of time slipping away. A desperate, wanton mewl escaped her as she clung to him. His hand slid down her back, pressing her closer, fitting her against him.

"Gemma," he groaned, tearing his mouth away, his cheek pressed to hers, his hot, hard breaths slipping into the whorls of her ear. "Tell me that we have an understanding."

Her understanding was that they were quite good at this. Last night seemed like a mere nightmare, and now she was awake and in this perfect dream. Her hands were in his hair again. She wasn't quite sure when that happened, but nevertheless…she used the position to angle his mouth back to hers.

He gave in for a moment, claiming her mouth on a greedy growl. But then he pulled back again, using kisses to punctuate his next words. "I'll speak to your aunt straightaway."

Because he was smiling, she couldn't stop her own, and ended up pressing her lips to his lips as well as to his teeth and chin. "Why are you going to speak to my aunt?"

"About our betrothal," he said, a deep satisfied rumble vibrating from his chest to hers.

It still took a moment before the words sunk in. When they finally did, she went stiff, breaking away from the kiss and turning her head. The painful truth tumbled out in a rush. "I cannot marry you."

He set her down on her feet in an instant and took a step back, withdrawing the warmth of his body. "You have given me every indication that you want"—he broke off and expelled a harsh breath—"that you are agreeable to the idea of marrying me."

Gemma closed her eyes as harsh reality seized her in its deathly cold grip. She wanted nothing else than to be his wife, but that would be a terrible betrayal to him. "I cannot escape the tarnish on my name and would not ruin yours with the association."

"You give Lady Tillmanshire too much power. I'm certain it is not as bad as you think."

The knot inside of her returned, now threaded with despair. "You do not understand. If it is not her, it will be someone else to take her place. And if I could, I would protect all whom I love from such slander." Lifting her gaze, she laid her hand on his arm, hoping to tell him in this small gesture that she counted him among those. "I am able to see things that you cannot."

He flinched and shrugged away from her touch, taking a step apart from her. "It is no wonder that your only thought is to escape. You only see blocked paths and barred doors, Gemma. Not the open arms right in front of you."

CHAPTER THIRTEEN

Sam returned to Dunnock Park with the weight of a desperate task on his shoulders. How could he convince Gemma that whatever people might say of her didn't matter to him?

The answer to that question, and a dozen others born in the same vein, would have to wait, however, because the Dowager Duchess of Vale was standing directly ahead of him in the corridor, clutching the missive in her hands.

"Have you seen her, Lord Ellery?" she asked, her voice shaking.

He could not help but push his own ragged nerves aside and soothe hers. "I have, and she appears to be well. If it helps, she did not tell me otherwise."

Her fretful gaze darted over his shoulder in the direction of the garden. "She has asked me not to go to her but only to ready the carriage. Even with only a garden between us, essentially she has separated herself from the people she is most fond of in the world."

Sam noted the error in her statement—*people*, instead of *person*—but did not speak it. Apparently, the dowager duchess was under the same misguided notion that he was. "What is in her heart, I cannot say. She refused my…invitation to return to the manor house. And I suspect she wishes to leave Dunnock Park altogether, as soon as possible."

When Sam saw that they were no longer alone in the corridor, he straightened his shoulders.

"Pardon the intrusion, m'lord, but I thought you'd want to hear this immediately," Mrs. Harkens said. "Lady Tillmanshire is above stairs and screeching about a lost brooch. And worse, she is blaming Miss Desmond, claiming to have found it in her bedchamber."

"*Impossible*," both Sam and the dowager duchess exclaimed at once. He'd returned the brooch directly to the baroness's room last night and placed it on the vanity beside her other jewelry. There was no way she could have missed it.

Unfortunately, he couldn't reveal what he'd done without implicating Gemma.

"No. No. No." The dowager duchess shook her head. "I do not believe it for an instant. There is something dastardly afoot, to be sure."

Mrs. Harkens nodded in agreement and waved her hand for a chambermaid, who was lurking off to the side, to step forward. "It's true, m'lord. Betsy confessed that she'd seen Miss Ashbury and Miss Leeds coming out of Miss Desmond's bedchamber."

"Are you certain of it, Betsy?" Sam asked.

The freckle-cheeked maid nodded. "I stayed in the shadow of the stairwell until they were gone, but it looked like they were up to no good, m'lord."

Fuming, Sam drew a breath between his teeth before responding. "Thank you both. I might require you to give this same testimony later this morning. Until then, send word to the stables to have Lady Tillmanshire's and Lady Cantham's carriages readied at once."

"Oh, my poor Gemma," the dowager duchess said, casting a stern glance toward the ceiling above her, as if to send a bolt of lightning down upon her enemies. "She has already had to deal with so much, living with a father who'd kept her from her family for so many years. When she was old enough to understand about his business dealings, he began locking her in their apartments and reading her correspondences to make sure that none of his own illicit actions would be discovered. All she'd wanted to do was escape it. And now she must be confronted with this heinous accusation?"

Sam was stunned. From their conversations, he knew that Gemma had had a less than conventional upbringing, but she'd never revealed to him how imprisoning it had been. Learning this, he could well understand her desire to flee. Who wouldn't, in her circumstance? And to add this boundless accusation…

He clenched his fists and gritted his teeth to keep from storming upstairs that instant. He thought he was angry before. Now he was enraged. *How dare they!*

"No," he said to the dowager duchess. "Miss Desmond will not have to worry. I will snuff this out once and for all."

She turned to leave but then hesitated and lifted her troubled gaze to him. "If my niece is determined to leave, I can only think of how that action will make it appear as if we are fleeing. The gossipmongers will not be kind to her."

"I will not allow that to happen," he vowed without knowing how, but only that he would do anything for Gemma. "I will come up with a plan to ensure her reputation is safe from further harm."

The dowager duchess offered a decisive nod. "Then you'll need time, and I'll make sure you get it."

Sam stormed down the corridor toward his study, cursing Albert Desmond under his breath.

Did that man even care about what Gemma would suffer because of his wrongdoings? Likely not. While Sam had been raised by the best of parents, she'd been left under the care of a self-serving criminal. And after all that, she still had to deal with the petty-mindedness of women like Lady Tillmanshire and Lady Cantham.

Sam wasn't pleased with his own behavior either. He shouldn't have lost his temper. He should have held on to his patience. He should have fallen at her feet and begged her forgiveness.

Out of the corner of his eye, he saw Holt stagger into the study after him.

Sam was in a vile temper and not fit for company. "Isn't it a bit early for you?"

"Why are you not in high spirits this morning?" Holt asked, sinking down into the overstuffed chair by the hearth. "I'd thought after engineering last night, your nauseatingly romantic heart would be bursting out of your waistcoat and your servants rushing around to prepare for your wedding."

Picking up the quill pen on his desk, he unintentionally snapped it between his fingers. Well, better it than Lady Tillmanshire's neck, he supposed. "Perhaps, if not for interference from another guest."

Sam withdrew another quill from the drawer and began to sharpen it with his penknife. It felt good to inflict violence on the tip, sending opaque shards scattering to the tidy surface of his desk.

"Would that be the same guest who is now upstairs bellowing about how Miss Desmond robbed her?" Holt asked.

Now this quill snapped too. Growling, he flicked a murderous gaze toward the ceiling. "That bitter baroness is attempting to sully Miss Desmond's reputation by branding her as a thief in order to dissuade my interest in her."

"Is this your own supposition or"—Holt stood and smoothed his hands down the front of his gray waistcoat— "are you taking Miss Desmond's word?"

Sam tossed down the broken quill and rounded the desk. "Just what are you implying?"

Holt shrugged in his usual indifferent manner, but his gaze was watchful. "During my sleepless hours, I finally remembered where I'd heard Miss Desmond's name before. I cannot remember the details, per se, but it was in association with Lord Markham."

Sam took another step until he was within strangling distance. "If you value our friendship and any of your teeth, do not speak another word."

"You're that sure of her character?" One dark brow lifted.

"I am," he said, with utter certainty pulsing through every vein.

"It's about bloody time." Holt clapped him on the shoulder and flashed a grin. "This self-doubt of yours has grown wearisome. And, by the by, I knew right away where I'd heard her name. You see, there was a tiny rumor that during Miss Desmond's first and, apparently, only attendance at a ball, Markham insulted her honor. Then, coincidentally, Markham broke both of his hands and fled London. No one knows for certain what happened. All I can say is that Miss Desmond must have friends. And any debutante who has a slew of people prepared to rally to her defense…well, she might be worthy of you."

Sam thought about the way he'd spoken to her this morning. It was unforgivable, especially after all that she had endured. "But am I worthy of her? When Gemma explained that she found Lady Tillmanshire's brooch in her room, I should have marched up to the baroness, handed her the bauble, and ordered her to leave immediately."

"And have the biddy wondering how you knew the brooch was in Miss Desmond's bedchamber?" Holt clucked his tongue but also waggled his eyebrows. "What happened to the brooch then?"

"I returned it to Lady Tillmanshire's chamber, of course. Then, this morning I learned from one of the chambermaids that Miss Ashbury and Miss Leeds were seen leaving Miss Desmond's room last night."

"Ah. So the rumors regarding their dogged determination to wreak havoc all Season were not overly exaggerated." He stopped with a quizzical arch of his brow. "What?"

"You were touring the continent, and yet you've heard more about the Season than I have. And I was there."

"It is your own fault for trying so hard to catch a bride that you paid no heed to rumors. Even when I am away, I keep my ears tuned to the buzz of society. How else do you catch an heiress, after all?" Holt cast a glance out the open doorway and toward the stairs, as if he were thinking of someone who wasn't quite an heiress but possessed a wealth of dimples. Then he shook his head, his expression resolute. "As for Miss Leeds and Miss Ashbury, apparently their alliance has sent many a tearful debutante rushing out of ballrooms and garden parties all Season."

"Then it's high time they got what they deserve." Suddenly Sam knew exactly what to do. Not only would it stop any chance that Lady Tillmanshire's accusations would hold any merit, but it might even free Gemma from the overwhelming desire to escape. "If you are willing, I could use your assistance."

"I am at your disposal."

"Ill?" Gemma repeated, to the marquess and marchioness. With her packed satchel waiting in the foyer, she'd assumed that Lord and Lady Russford had called her into the parlor to bid her farewell, not to tell her about Aunt Edith's sudden illness.

Although, knowing her aunt's tendency to believe herself a matchmaker, Gemma was skeptical. "In her note this morning, my aunt said she was prepared to depart at once."

Lady Russford shifted her eyes to her husband. "Yes, well, apparently her illness was rather sudden."

"But slight," Lord Russford added carefully. "Nothing to worry about."

"Just something that would make it uncomfortable to travel," Lady Russford added, a little too brightly and received an encouraging nod from her husband.

If Gemma were watching them at a gaming table, she'd believe they both had cards up their sleeves. Yet while her suspicions were on alert, she wasn't certain what their intentions were.

"Then I should go to her, I suppose." Yet at the thought of returning to the manor house, where Sam was right this instant, her heart and stomach began to turn in opposite directions. She didn't think she could face him.

"No, no, no," Lady Russford said quickly. "You mustn't just yet. According to her maid, the dowager duchess wishes for no visitors at this time."

Lord Russford nodded agreement. "And of course you are more than welcome to stay here."

"In fact, we insist upon it."

Gemma wasn't certain what to make of this development. Though perhaps she'd read them wrong from the start and they were only being nice. And perhaps Aunt Edith truly was too ill to travel. It might have been something she ate at breakfast. Gemma wouldn't put it past Lady Cantham to slip soured milk into someone's tea.

Resigned, Gemma offered a smile. "You are both too kind. I feel as if I wore out my welcome hours ago."

"Nonsense. Mr. Wortham and I are glad for the company. In the meantime, would you like to help me finish the counterpane?"

"Miss Desmond is a thief, just like her father," Lady Tillmanshire declared with a haughty sniff, her coterie nodding in agreement. Lady Cantham, Miss Ashbury, and Miss Leeds all gathered around her in his study with their noses in the air.

Sam did his best to subdue his urge to have them escorted from his house. That would come soon enough, but first he would protect Gemma from their slander. "I will ask you politely, and only once, to recant your unfounded accusation."

"*Unfounded?*" Lady Tillmanshire blustered. "That good-for-nothing girl crept into my room in the dead of night to steal from—"

"Impossible," Sam interrupted. "Miss Desmond was not even here last night. In fact, she is a guest of my parents in the dower house."

Lady Tillmanshire's mouth opened and closed like a fish in need of water. "The...the dower house? But that just cannot be. You said on the first night that you would not introduce any of the guests to your parents until...you had reached...an understanding."

"Precisely," he said, looking out the open study door to see a team of footmen carrying down their luggage to be strapped to the waiting carriages. Then he cut directly to the point. "You are no longer a guest at Dunnock Park, Lady Tillmanshire.

"You may not know this, but the *ton* has a low opinion of those who sling about false accusations of this enormity. They are especially unforgiving of upstarts who reek of new money and parade themselves about town in gilded carriages that they can no longer afford." He took a moment for his words to sink in. "Oh yes, the secret of your strained finances is on the lips of many. Out of pity, I ignored those rumors, wanting to give fairness due to you and your daughter."

"And for that we humbly thank you," Lady Tillmanshire said in a rush, likely not noticing how Lady Cantham took hold of her stepdaughter's arm and retreated a step, their faces pinched in haughty disdain.

"The truth of the matter is, I was wrong to do so. I see that now," he continued, as if the baroness hadn't spoken. "Regardless, I have kindly made arrangements for your room and board."

"You are too generous," she said with a sigh of relief. "Are we, perhaps, to stay at the dower house as well?"

He was astounded by her amount of gall. "No. I have arranged for you to reside with your daughter's betrothed, Lord Haggerty."

The four of them gasped in revulsion, as they should. The man was beyond vile, his character lacking in every gentlemanly courtesy. It seemed fitting for the baron to marry into a family that possessed the same qualities—or lack thereof.

"I have learned that—contrary to what you have told me, Lady Tillmanshire—your daughter is still very much betrothed to Lord Haggerty. Since his estate is only a few miles from here, I have sent a missive to him that he should expect his bride's family this very day."

Miss Ashbury's skin paled, tinged with a yellowish green. "Mother, I cannot marry him. He is so hideous that I can hardly stand the look of him."

"And you will not marry him if I have anything to say about it." The baroness turned to Sam, advancing in small, desperate shuffles. "Lord Haggerty lied to us about his fortune. The truth is that he is nothing more than a pauper, claiming that he possessed a great estate and fortune. We never would have considered him otherwise."

Sam felt no pity but merely shrugged. "Sadly, society is used to lies of this sort. There are far worse crimes than being poor, such as"—he offered a pointed look to Miss Ashbury—"crying off after a betrothal. A young woman who does such a thing is labeled a jilt, which most often ensures a life of spinsterhood."

Then Sam turned on the other two. "As for you, Lady Cantham and Miss Leeds, my servants have informed me that you were willing participants in the scheme to brand Miss Desmond a thief." He walked to the door and gestured for them to depart. "And I have ordered your carriage as well."

Lady Tillmanshire stopped, her voice rising with affront as she pointed a finger at Lady Cantham. "Is that all the reprimand she's to receive? The stolen brooch was her idea."

"So you say," Lady Cantham said, lifting a hand to smooth her pale hair, "but who is going to believe you any longer? You've lost your fortune, and your daughter is marrying a pauper."

Miss Leeds and her stepmother exchanged a look and snickered.

Suddenly, Miss Ashbury launched herself at Miss Leeds, claws at the ready. "And you will be a spinster because no gentleman will have you once I reveal the truth about you and your riding master!"

Then all four of the women fell on each other, brawling in the foyer. It was a pitiful display of scratching and screeching, of flying hair ribbons and ripped sashes. He even saw a brown wig skid across the floor and noted that it belonged to Lady Tillmanshire.

Sam rolled his eyes and ordered the footmen to carry the melee outside and then to bolt the doors.

Swaggering down the hall, Holt chuckled. "House parties are far more amusing than I ever imagined. Perhaps I should host my own after my father's imminent wake."

"I fear I cannot yet recommend it." But if all this gained him Gemma, then it would be well worth it. As for now, he was waiting to see if his plan would work. With the help of Holt, the Hollander twins, and Gemma's aunt, they'd written to many of their closest allies and influential members of society. "Did you send the letters?"

"Indeed. The Dowager Duchess of Vale and *One* and *Two* have all sent theirs to be posted in the village, while I sent mine with my valet to be hand-delivered. I imagine a few responses, from those living nearby, will come as soon as tomorrow."

Sam hoped Holt was right. If everything went as it should, Gemma wouldn't need to worry that her father's deeds had tarnished her reputation beyond repair. If people took the time to know her, they would be as besotted as he was. All she needed was an opportunity to show them who she was.

Then, perhaps, she wouldn't feel the need to escape after all.

CHAPTER FOURTEEN

"So many invitations, my dear. I do not know which of them we should accept first," Aunt Edith said from her bed-chamber in the manor house later that week. As usual, her silvery coiffure was immaculate, and behind her, a towering placement of pillows, so that she was reclining in the perfect pose.

Gemma looked through the open door toward the corridor when she heard the sound of footsteps. Her pulse quickened at her wrists and at the base of her throat, wondering if she would finally see Sam.

But when she saw it was only a footman, she turned back to her aunt, feeling an empty ache inside. It only worsened as she stared down at the stack of letters on the bedside table.

It was foolish to feel this overwhelming despondency, she knew. After all, she should be glad that dozens of letters had arrived in the past couples of days, each of them expressing a fervent desire to have Aunt Edith *and* Gemma pay a call on them. It seemed as if she no longer had to worry about her reputation.

She knew this was Sam's doing. Only he would have been so thoughtful, ensuring that her life altered for the better before she left.

She should be ecstatic. At last, she could move forward without being a burden to her family. She could have the quiet life she always wanted.

"Though perhaps it would be best to stay with Northcliff and Ivy and be present when the baby arrives," Aunt Edith continued. "Then, by early next spring, we could travel to Liam and Adeline for their first bundle. Between your cousins, we may be well exhausted from travel and up to our necks in infants." She laughed fondly, shuffling from one letter to the next, heedless of how the world had suddenly stopped spinning. "Oh, and here is a delightful one from my friend Lady Cosgrove. She writes, 'I am abundantly pleased to report that Lilah is in a delicate condition and fairly glowing. As for her husband, you would hardly recognize Jack. While he is fierce as a lion, he is as gentle as a lamb with her and has taken well to his new situation as Viscount Locke.'"

"I am happy for them," Gemma said absently. "Each time I've spoken with Lilah, she has been more than kind. She even helped me finish painting the mural in Ivy's nursery."

Aunt Edith sat straighter and held up her finger. "I just thought of something. I seem to recall that Lilah was the one who Lord Ellery had courted early this last Season. Oh, but I believe her heart was already engaged. Though apparently his was not, for I daresay, he would have been too forlorn to continue his search for a bride and host this party. Men tend to pine and brood when their hearts are bruised."

Gemma remembered what Lady Russford had said about Sam's having been cast aside before, and a swift spark of jealousy ignited over the notion of Lilah winning Sam's favor. "He has the nature to recover easily, I think. By next Season, he will surely fix his attention on someone else."

Proof of that was the way he'd kept his distance from Gemma, as if there'd never been anything between them. They hadn't spoken for three days, not since he accused her of seeing only closed doors. Which, in her mind, was rather ironic, considering how he'd so efficiently closed the door on her. And coming here, crossing the garden from the dower house to the manor, had not been easy for her. She'd fretted over seeing him again and what she might say. Yet he'd been conveniently absent each time she'd visited her aunt.

That ache welled inside her.

Aunt Edith shook her head. "Apparently, his *nature*, as you put it, has altered, for I heard from Lady Russford this very morning that her son has abandoned his quest indefinitely. Lord Stapleton and Miss Stapleton have left this morning, as have the Misses Creighton. Such a shame too. Lord Ellery would have made a fine husband."

Gemma swallowed down a rise of emotion that clogged her throat. "The finest."

"Oh, look here," Aunt Edith said, back to her reading, "Lady Cosgrove continues with this interesting tidbit about Juliet. Even though she and Lord Thayne are still on their honeymoon, they asked Zinnia, as well as Marjorie Harwick, to oversee the delivery of a rather large crate to their own library. And do you know what was inside? A red velvet chaise longue. What do you think they would need with such an uncommon piece of furniture in the library? It raises an eyebrow, does it not?"

Gemma wasn't paying attention. She was staring ruefully down at one of the invitations in her hand. "He went through so much effort so that I could leave."

"My dear." Paper crinkling in her lap, Aunt Edith leaned forward and covered Gemma's hand. "Do you not think it possible that he was trying to make it easier for you to stay?"

"If that were true then one of these invitations would be from him." Or in the very least, he would have come to see her. Instead, he plagued her with his absence each night by leaving a woodbine blossom on the pillow in her bedchamber at the dower cottage. She didn't even know how he was doing it. But it was cruel reminder, nonetheless, of what she might have had if things were different. She shook her head. "Not that it matters in the end."

"Why do you say that?"

"Because the moment my father returns or is caught in some scheme halfway around the world, then all of this will be for naught. The name of Desmond will be cast in the gutter once more, and anyone associated with it will be as well."

Aunt Edith remained silent through Gemma's rant, her expression thoughtful, searching. "I cannot believe I never noticed it before now. But your mother—rest her sweet soul—did this very thing whenever she was frightened. When I first married her brother, she was still in the schoolroom. Often on my visits, she would conjure up terrifying tales of all the monstrous things that might be inside her wardrobe or beneath her bed. I thought she was trying to frighten me or impress me with her dramatic skills. It was only later that

I realized she needed to imagine the worst possibility in order to protect herself from…oh, whatever creepy-crawly might have been lurking in the shadows. It was her means of garnering courage, I suppose."

Even though Gemma enjoyed the story, she was not fond of the point her aunt was making. "I'm not imagining things. I know this will happen when my father returns."

Aunt Edith drew in a breath and said gently, "Dearest, he has no intention of returning. Not ever."

"Forgive me, Aunt, but you could not possibly know this. He has always done whatever he chooses without thought or care for anyone else," she said, her voice brittle.

"Precisely." Then Aunt Edith looked down to the coral strand around Gemma's neck. "That necklace *was* your mother's. I'd been holding onto it for a time, waiting for the right moment."

"But how"—Gemma touched the beads, half expecting them to disappear like a mirage or part of a dream—"did you find it?"

"Your father sold it shortly after your mother's death." Her mouth tightened. "Thankfully, the London jeweler recognized the unique clasp and sent me a missive. I purchased it and have had it ever since, in safekeeping for you. Your mother wanted you to have it, as with all her jewelry."

Gemma inhaled a shaky breath, garnering her own courage for what she had to say. "But I lost—*sold* all of it in a market. It was terrible, and I will never forgive myself."

"But you couldn't have, my dear. Your father had sold every bit of your mother's jewelry before he took you away from me and left London. Then he tried to hide what he'd done by replacing them with replicas—real jewels with paste and the gold with brass."

Stunned, Gemma lifted her face. All this time, all these years, she'd been tormented by that day in the market. "They weren't even hers?"

Aunt Edith shook her head and brushed a hand over Gemma's cheek. "If I'd have known you thought that, I would have told you much sooner. I admit that I carry a great deal of guilt of my own. I spent years allowing your father to siphon money from me with the threat that he would cut off my contact with you if I didn't. What I should have done instead was to gather an army and find you for myself."

"And how would you have known where to find me? We were never in one place for more than a week," Gemma said distractedly, as a sense of new awareness was awakening. She'd always wondered why she'd been allowed to write her aunt. Father had always been paranoid that she would say something in her letters about his business dealings. He often threatened to cut off Gemma's contact with Aunt Edith if she ever exposed him. Now she knew that he'd been doing the same to both of them. "Why do you suppose he finally brought me back to London?"

"When you turned twenty, I stopped paying him. I'd thought—hoped, rather—that he might come to me for money and bring you back to London with him. It was a risk, I knew. But I had to do something. You sounded so lonely in your letters."

Suddenly, Gemma knew it was true—her father wasn't coming back. There was no longer any profit in it for him.

Though, truth be told, she'd suspected this all along. In fact, years ago she'd reconciled herself to the fact that her

father had never truly loved her. He'd always been more con-
cerned with money and his forgeries than he had been with
his daughter.

It was strange that this confirmation didn't distress her.
In fact, having proof of it was…well, fairly liberating. She
took a deep breath and thought of this moment as a single
stitch in a long row.

"You're right. I was lonely." Rising from the bedside chair,
she embraced her aunt, pressing a kiss to her cheek. "And I'm
glad you made that decision."

Then, glancing at the mirror stand, Gemma touched the
necklace. It was as if her mother were here. In that instant,
she could almost see a memory of her, just a brief ghost of a
glimpse. "Did she have the habit of covering her mouth when
she laughed?"

A soft smile touched Aunt Edith's lips as she dabbed
away the wetness from beneath her eyes. "Oh yes. I'd forgotten that. You see, she had a chipped tooth—a small bit of
nothing in the corner that you couldn't even see. I don't think
she ever knew how beautiful she was. You're like her in that
regard as well, though I think there's a certain viscount who
is very much aware it."

Gemma pondered that statement, unsure. "Do you really
think I'm guilty of imagining the worst as a way to protect
myself?"

Aunt Edith didn't say anything but patted Gemma's hand.

Strange. Gemma thought she was so clever at reading
other people, but she never thought she was hiding something this monumental up her own sleeve. "Truth be told, I'm

not certain which is more frightening—imagining the worst thing that could possibly happen or wishing for the best."

"Well, I think you've done enough of one, and it's time to try the other." Then Aunt Edith swept the coverlet aside and stepped out of bed. "I'm feeling much better all of a sudden. What do you think, my dear? Should I order a carriage, or would you like to stay?"

Sam stood on the bank of the pond, agitated and wondering if patience could kill a man. It had been three days since he'd spoken with Gemma. Three days since he'd touched her, kissed her. Three days since he'd set a plan in motion to give her the choice of having the life she wanted. The only problem was, he didn't know if she wanted him. And the waiting was slowly killing him.

He decided that he did not like falling in love at all. It was a wretched, restless feeling that brought a sharp, searing pain to each beat of his heart and made his lungs burn with every effort to breathe.

Before, when he'd courted Lilah, he'd imagined being able to grow into love eventually. Given the number of things they had in common, he felt that he would have been pleasantly content with his life. But this was far different.

When he thought of Gemma, he didn't just see contentment and amiable conversation. He saw his life, all of it— hour by hour and day by day—spanning decades. He saw himself waking up to her face each morning and kissing her before bed each night. He saw their hands intertwined as they peered down into the cradle of their firstborn. He saw the way her smile would change over time, adding wrinkle by wrinkle, her hair threading with silver. And he wanted that— no, he *needed* that. He needed to spend his life with her. And he knew that no one else would ever compare.

Yet he also knew that he could not force her to want the same thing. He could not make her choose a life with him. Or to love him.

Losing interest in the sport of angling, he dropped his ash wood pole to the ground, allowing his line to sink, untended, into the depths. Standing there for a time, he stared out across the glimmering surface, kneading a fist over the gnawing ache in the center of his chest. He wondered if it would ever abate. But mostly, he wished the remedy he sought would suddenly appear, the way she had that first day.

While his mind was preoccupied with that memory, he noticed a movement out of the corner of his eye as his pole began to slide to the water's edge. But no, not slide; it was being pulled.

Sam quickly reached for the pole, his fist tight on the cork grip. He reared back, taking hold of the line and hauling the tip out of the water in one deft movement. But he was jerked forward toward the water's edge. Whatever was on the other end was looking for a fight. Digging the heels of his Hessians into the soft earth, Sam was ready to give it to him.

For a quarter of an hour, the titanic beast gave Sam his best, leading him down the edge of the pond toward the bottleneck. Then, after one last hard struggle, one final jerk, the monster broke free of the surface, twisting his long, slender body in the air, the sun glinting off his dark green-blue scales.

There he was—the pike.

Sam couldn't believe it. For years this fish had remained elusive, had dodged every attempt he'd made to catch him. This was the moment he'd been waiting for.

"At last, I have caught you," Sam said, hauling him to shore. Yet when he looked into the pike's eyes, he felt no measure of triumph. He only thought of how much he wished Gemma were here with him, her laughter skimming across the surface of the pond. "Sadly, my friend, I would much rather have caught her instead."

Careful of the jagged rows of sharp teeth, Sam removed his hook and tossed the pike back into the water. The pike lingered for a moment, going still in the shallows, and seemed to look back at Sam as if he too were disappointed by this anticlimactic end to their battle.

Then he swam off with a lazy flick of his spiked fin—a taunt, daring Sam to try to catch him again. Instead, Sam wrapped his line around the pole and laid it in the grass. But when he stood, he caught a movement across the water.

Turning his gaze, he saw Gemma standing on the opposite bank, her hands clasped beneath the sash of her rose-colored muslin. He blinked, believing her to be an apparition.

"Was that the elusive Mr. Pike?" she asked, her soft voice reaching him over the water, her eyes watchful and uncertain.

"It was." Standing still, he could not look away, just in case he was hallucinating. If this was a dream, he did not want to awaken.

She lowered her hands to pick up her skirt as she began to walk along the edge. "When I was a child, I once met a gambler who wore a pike tooth around his neck. He believed it brought him luck. He always claimed that if you caught a pike and set him free, he would grant your wish."

Sam might very well believe that too. But it depended on what happened in the upcoming minutes. "The truth of pikes?"

"You could say that," she replied, the hint of a smile on her lips, her focus on navigating past the few stones and clusters of tall grasses that marked her path. "I can understand how grateful the pike must feel to be set free. That was all I wanted, after all. For years it seemed to be as elusive as your friend." Then she paused and met his gaze. "Thanks to you, I have the freedom to live my life without bringing censure upon my family."

Was that the reason she was here? If so, then her gratitude was a harsh reminder that if she left, it would be his own fault.

If she hadn't had another choice, then she might have married him, even if only to salvage her reputation. And yet he wanted more from her—and *for* her—than that. He wanted her happiness and to see all the days of her life joined with his. Above all, he wanted her heart open to love. And he would fill it, each minute of every day.

"But then I realized," she continued, taking a few more tentative steps toward him, "that if I could choose to live anywhere on earth, I could think of no better place than Dunnock Park."

His heart pounded faster, beating against the withered husk of uncertainty. Yet he told that organ not to rush ahead. After all, she might still be here to say farewell but merely wanted to ease into it by complimenting his grounds.

All right, perhaps that was a ridiculous assumption, but he refused to assume she loved him before she said the words.

"It is a fair prospect, I grant you," he said with a casual sweep of his arm over the vista as he began to walk around the bend toward her. By another feat of patience, he kept his pace moderate, meandering.

She frowned as if she hadn't expected that response. "Yes, well…I suppose it would be too bold of me to ask if I could live in a little one-room cottage, right here, nestled within the woodbines?"

"Somewhat bold," he mused. "Especially if you want me to build it. After all, constructing a proper cottage, even a small one, would take months, perhaps even years. In the meantime, where would you live?"

"I"—she swallowed—"I would hope to live nearby."

She was so careful and cautious that it was driving him mad. He feared he might die from anticipation before he reached her. "But why—if you no longer need to worry about your surname and could live anywhere in the world—would you wish to live near Dunnock Park?"

"Because my heart is here," she said on a shallow breath, her breasts rising and falling in rapid succession as she searched his gaze.

The air grew thicker with expectation, and he found his own breathing labored. "Are you speaking as a philosopher?"

"The truth of falling in love is that you can no longer imagine your life without that person."

"Forgive me, I didn't quite catch that," he said as joy tumbled through him. "The breeze must have carried it away."

She shook her head at first, then pressed her lips together as if to keep from grinning back at him, but the happiness glistening in her eyes gave her away. "I love you."

He couldn't help it—he let out a wondrous laugh as he closed the distance between them, every last doubt leaving him. Then he took her small hands in his. "I've been waiting ages to hear you say that. I knew from the day we met that I loved you. That you belonged here with me."

She gave him her smile, her face glowing with unguarded happiness. "I have a confession to make. I've known for quite some time too. In fact, from that very first day I've had the startling impulse to fling my arms wide and then wrap myself around you."

He liked the sound of that. "Show me."

Without hesitation, she leapt into his arms and began to pepper kisses over his face and jaw. "Do you think *this* would have been too bold for a first meeting?"

"I think your aunt would have wielded her parasol to separate us," he said, his mouth finding hers. He held her tightly, his hands and body greedy for the feel of her against him.

A small, effortless laugh escaped Gemma. "No, indeed. She would have pulled the carriage around and driven us to the nearest chapel, grinning madly all the while."

"The nearest one is in Banfern Glenn." He drew back just enough to gauge her reaction. The last time he brought up marriage, he didn't receive the reaction he'd expected.

She pursed her lips in thought, taunting him with that plump bottom one. "Such a short distance. In essence, you'd be free to marry whenever you chose after the banns were read, or…"

"I would purchase a special license." He felt the smallest hitch in her breathing, but her expression revealed little.

"Hmm. You must be quite certain of your bride to know that she would be amenable to a hasty wedding."

Was the minx trying to keep him guessing? He retaliated by rasping his lips across hers and nuzzling into each upturned corner of her mouth. Feeling the corresponding tremble through her body, he only continued his onslaught. "I would offer her some enticements to persuade her."

"Your strong arms around her? Slow, melting kisses?" she asked against his lips, nibbling softly and making him wonder who was seducing whom. "Though, if she truly loved you, the only enticement that she would need would be to know that you were hers."

For clarification, he kissed her again, fully, slowly sinking down onto the cool grass, the air thick and sweet with the scent of woodbine. "I am yours, Gemma. But more importantly, you are mine."

"Coincidentally," she began, lying half beneath him and threading her fingers in his hair, "your wedding counterpane was finished this morning. I put the last stitch in it myself."

Imagining her lying beneath it, he gave her another lingering kiss, his hands drifting over her waist to the curve of her hip. Then he lifted his head and winked at her. "Then I suppose it's high time I find a wife."

Her eyes narrowed, glinting in playful warning. "Did you know there is an old Dunnock Park custom that states you must ask the woman who puts the final stitch in your wedding counterpane to marry you?"

"I don't believe I've heard that one," he said, intending to ask her as soon as he kissed her once more. The best part of it all was that he knew she would say yes. "When, precisely, did this begin?"

She smiled against his lips. "Ages and ages ago."

EPILOGUE

December 1825

"How do you like Woodbine Cottage, my lady?"

A happy laugh escaped Gemma, turning into puffs of vapor in the frostbitten air. On the other side of the still, mirrored surface of the pond, the little stone structure looked snug and inviting. It rested beyond the willow, contentedly nestled between a pair of evergreens, with a curl of smoke rising from the chimney that poked through the thatched roof.

"Is this truly for me?" She lifted her gaze to Sam, still feeling as if this were part of a dream. One she'd been living since summer.

Holding her hand, he tugged her into his embrace, pulling her flush against him through the layers of their winter clothing. "You asked if you could live in a one-room cottage at Dunnock Park. And I will always give you what you want."

"As I recall very well from last night." She grinned unabashedly, slipping her arms inside his greatcoat and earned a rakish grin from her husband. "Though surely you're not going to make me live here. After all, I've grown quite accustomed to having a close proximity to the master of Dunnock Manor."

As it was, they couldn't make it an entire day without one of them tugging the other into the nearest room. The delicious truth of marrying an irresistible man.

He gave her a playful glower as he worked the top button of her redingote free and then the second one. "I'll only send you here when you are bad and pretend to lose when we are playing cards."

She sighed as he nuzzled the corner of her mouth. He nipped her chin and skimmed along the underside of her jaw. She tilted her head to allow him better access. "Can I help it if I enjoy the many ways you console me when I lose?"

"I rather like those as well." Deftly unfastening the entire row of buttons, he slipped inside. His gloved hands surrounded her ribcage, thumbs beneath her swollen breasts, teasing her in slow, climbing sweeps as his mouth heated a path down her exposed throat.

Having experienced the wonders he could perform with his mouth, hands, and all of his other impressive parts, her body clenched in a damp, expectant rush. "Sam, take me to the cottage."

"Afraid of scandalizing the woodland creatures"—his lips curved against her flesh, his voice a seductive murmur—"again?"

"Perhaps I'm merely eager to give you my present." She slipped her hand between them, pressing her palm along the thick length of him until he was out of breath, his forehead pressed to hers and his eyes dark and drowsy. It was his own fault for unlocking the wild, hungry side of her nature. She couldn't get enough of him.

They wasted no more time, their hurried footsteps crackling across the crystallized grass. And when he opened the door, a shower of dried woodbine petals rained down like wedding confetti, littering the floor of the snug cottage. Peering up, she saw that he'd rigged a basket overhead to spill when she entered. When she looked at him, he offered a shrug, a lopsided grin on his lips.

"I hope you know that I love you." So full of joy, she couldn't stop herself from launching into his arms.

He caught her handily, closing the door with his foot, and brushing his lips over hers. "I have an inkling."

Then they were alone, closed inside this cozy space, the air sweetly scented and warmed by the flickering fire in the small half-circle hearth. She wanted to explore every detail…but later. Now, she only wanted him.

Sam shared her thoughts, ridding her of her redingote, and biting off his gloves before his hand slipped to the nape of her neck, drawing her mouth to his.

They'd become quite good at undressing each other. It was like a hurried game of *expose and kiss.* Her lips explored him, first beneath his cravat where a faint line of stubble met smooth, warm flesh. Followed by the hard protrusion of his Adam's apple. The ridge of his clavicle where his shirt fell open. Then his waistcoat was gone, followed by his shirt, sailing overhead to land unheeded on the floor. She leaned close, her lips tingling as they swept over the smattering of crisp blond hair over his chest. A flat brown nipple. The firm bulge of a bicep.

Divesting her of her dress and her worsted petticoat, he picked her up against him, fitting her hips in perfect alignment with his. She became acutely aware of the suede texture of his still-fastened breeches along her inner thighs, and she couldn't stop herself from clamping tighter around him. And with the hard summit of his erection, he teased the taut, pulsing bundle of nerves at her sex into a frenzy.

Her hips hitched, the pressure giving a sweet stab of pleasure. He wasn't playing fair. At this rate, she would reach her own pinnacle before he was even inside her. She had to remedy that at once.

He turned around, pressing her against the door, his hand behind her head, cushioning her. Anchored by his lean, solid body, she reached down and nimbly freed him, his flesh heavy and scorching in her grasp. A few errant woodbine petals tumbled around them as she positioned him. Even though she was wet and eager, he stretched her fully, his thick flesh edging inside her in slow-burning, unhurried degrees. She could feel her walls closing around him, shrinking, clutching. Her back arched, reaching toward the crest of her own pleasure, seeking immediate release. Then, just as she felt her body cleaving to his, he went still.

Wedged inside her, Sam pressed his temple to hers, a faint sheen of perspiration shared between them. "Not yet, my love. If you go over the edge, I'll surely follow."

The thought of him losing himself sent an uncontrollable tremor through her, and one swift clench.

He groaned, his chest shuddering on a breath as he gave her a look of heated warning. She bit down on her lip to keep from grinning, knowing that neither of them would last long.

Proof of that was the way he took her mouth, devouring her. "Give me that grin, Gemma. I want to taste it."

And she did, right before he rocked against her, seated fully inside her. She gasped as he withdrew and pitched forward, his thrusts in and in, so deep she was surprised she didn't combust from pleasure. It kept building higher, so high it was hard to breathe. She broke from their kiss, her teeth sinking down onto his shoulder, holding on until—

She cried out, her body quaking, sparks lighting up behind her clenched eyes. Sam answered with a surprised shout, hips driving faster, endlessly, prolonging her shudders until he'd claimed every last one. Then he slowed, whispering a series of low, wanton murmurs, their bodies slick with pleasure.

Spent and blissful, they soon found themselves on an untidy pile of clothes. And they continued their game of *expose and kiss* but at a more leisurely, satisfied pace.

"Thank you for my cottage," she said, lifting her head and lying half atop him, her leg gliding sinuously between his. "It's the perfect size for the two of us."

He reached up to tuck a wayward curl behind her ear, his eyes glowing in the firelight, a smile on his lips. "Rather short-sighted of me, considering..."

"Considering what?" she asked when he didn't continue. Narrowing her eyes, she studied him closely. When she saw the tender way he gazed at her, she realized he knew her secret. "I wasn't going to tell you until Christmas morning. The news is supposed to be your present."

He shifted, turning them until she was lying back on his greatcoat. Propped up on his elbow, his hand brushed her cheek and skimmed down her body, pausing to mold around one of her plump breasts. "And I'm to wait until…June, I suppose…before this present arrives?"

Hmph. "For a man who claimed an uncertainty for reading people, you seem to have developed quite a knack for it."

"Only because I find the object of my study utterly fascinating." He kissed her softly, lingering. "Besides, was I supposed to miss the fact that your perfect nipples are slightly darker and so sensitive that I need only blow on them to bring them to a hard peak?" He paused to prove his point with a thin stream of air over the tip, and drew out a gasp from her, head back, her body bowing toward him. Then he moved lower, his hand splayed over her abdomen. Bending down, he kissed her there, gently, reverently. "And was I not supposed to notice how your slender stomach is firmer and with the faintest rounded swell, where my child is growing inside of you?"

She threaded her fingers in his hair, transfixed by a wave of such happiness that her eyes misted with tears. "I suppose I'll have to find new ways to surprise you over the next few decades."

He moved over her, pressed his lips to hers again, and grinned. "I look forward to it."

Acknowledgments

As I mentioned in the dedication, this book would not have been possible without the fans who wanted a happily ever after for Ellery. But I also need to thank my editor, Nicole Fischer, for her insight and commitment to making the story shine. Getting through the editing process is a lot more fun when there are smiley faces and *lol*s in the margins.

Many thanks go out to my agent, Stefanie Lieberman, for working her negotiating magic on this contract and making sure that even the side characters receive their happy endings.

To the baristas who only know me as the *crazy cozy lady*, thank you for enabling my chai addiction.

Writing this book has been another dream come true. Like many authors, I am an introvert who works best in solitude. Yet any worthwhile endeavor requires balance, and I am forever grateful for the warmth and support I receive from the outside world and from the strength I gain from my ever-present faith in God.

Thank you, all, for welcoming this story into your hearts.

Want more beautiful love stories from Vivienne Lorret?
Well, you're in luck!

Keep an eye out for a brand new Regency
romance series about three matchmaking sisters
who live by one rule: never fall for the clients!
But you know what they say about best-laid plans…

HOW TO FORGET A DUKE

Coming Spring 2018 from Avon Books!

USA Today bestselling author **VIVIENNE LORRET** transforms copious amounts of tea into words. She is an Avon Impulse author of works including the Wallflower Wedding series, the Rakes of Fallow Hall series, the Season's Original series, and the upcoming Emma Identity series. For more information on her books, sign up for her newsletter at www.vivlorret.net.

Discover great authors, exclusive offers, and more at hc.com.

Dear Reader,

I hope you liked the latest romance from Avon Impulse! If you're looking for another steamy, fun, emotional read, be sure to check out some of our upcoming titles.

First up we have a delightful new story compilation from superstar Eloisa James! A MIDSUMMER NIGHT'S DIS-GRACE AND OTHER STORIES includes a short but sweet dip into the world of her beloved Essex Sisters, as well as other Cinderella-themed novellas! Eloisa always delivers witty, charming reads and this collection is no different!

We also have a brand new series from Mia Sosa for all you contemporary romance fans! Mia makes her Avon Impulse debut with ACTING ON IMPULSE, a fun, flirty (and a little dirty) novel about a Hollywood heartthrob who meets the woman of his dreams on an airplane...except she doesn't recognize him! Sparks may fly, but what will happen when she finds out the truth? You'll have to read this sexy, diverse romantic comedy to find out!

You can purchase any of these titles by clicking the links above or by visiting our website, www.AvonRomance.com. Thank you for loving romance as much as we do...enjoy!

Sincerely,
Nicole Fischer
Editorial Director
Avon Impulse